Also by the author

The JFK Order
Banquo's Safe

Myth Politic

AE Reiff

Histericks 24

Contents

Acknowledgments

Isaiah **in America, The** *Fairie Queene* **Cometh** interprets the new Reichstag Resolution of the joint American Government, September 12, 2001 when Speaker Daschle insisted out of his own mouth that Jerusalem and Washington, Isaiah and America were one. How this played in the eyes of the storied "American people" is interpreted in **Oracle Weimar** where the psyche of a German general's son studying at Oxford, Horst Keller, at the beginning of the Nazi takeover, encounters poet Stephen Spender. Spender inscribed his *Poems* of 1933 to Keller twelve days after the Reichstag fire of 27 Feb 1933, and made further mention of him in his Journals. When the German parliament burned to the ground, Nazi leadership used that fire to overwhelm constitutional protections, to prevent against "terrorism." If that sounds as familiar as the aftermath of the Twin Towers of the World Trade Center, America's leaders claimed they needed a "Pearl Harbor event" to begin the terror of their wars of proxy all over the world and overwhelm the American constitution. The isolated, quiescent psychology of Horst Keller foreshadows the "American people." Weimar thus predicts America. Spender "saw beneath the surface…a restlessness that never ceased." (Spender, *Journals, 1939-1983*. 30). In *A Tale of Two Towers* New Directions publisher, James Laughlin, in "Above the City," presages airplanes hitting towers and their fall in 1946. How seriously we should take this is evidenced by another poet, Wendell Berry, debunking it in service to dis-Intelligence. The idea of disinformation is that narratives are made to mislead attention away from the obvious, like why a Secret Service counter sniper waited to eliminate the Trump gunman until after 7 shots had been fired. If some one "accidently" foresees all or part of the underground event, like Laughlin here, or Trump turns his head just in time for the miss, its hirelings ameliorate responsibility. No deniability however is offered for the horror of the **Pergamon Altar at the 2008 Denver Convention**, where an American President is nominated from the center of a holographic Ishtar Gate of Babylon. The Ishtar Gate was the 8th gate into Babylon that Jewish captives passed through into captivity in the fifth century B.C., symbolic of the multiple layers of American captivity since. The Pergamon Altar appears in the biblical book of *Revelation* as the place "where Satan's throne is…where Satan dwells" (*Revelation* 2.11). Both artifacts stolen by the Germans were toured by Obama in Berlin immediately before touting them. To further represent this supernatural myth politic Samuel Taylor Coleridge's opium poem of Kubla Khan connects to this delirium in **Opiomes, The Domes**.Most of these appeared to much fanfare at *Red Fez* along with **Space Alien Politics** and **Satan at the Super Collider.** In Space Alien, General MacArthur warns West Point cadets of planetary war just as Phil Schneider is rappelling the Dulce Archuleta to confront the alien bases after building them. The predictions of September are prepared before in **Satan at the Super Collider,** seen in Canto 34 of Dante's *Inferno,* along with **Hybrid Beastiary***,* science camouflaged as fiction, the beginnings of hybrid chimeras. **Melt***,* of Antarctica, is the *Red Fez* grand finale, the last to clear that "culture of consensus," detailing that night of the election of Donald Trump when Secretary of State John Kerry flew to Antarctica. In one week that winter, Feb 11 to 18 2016, this unlikely chain of events occurred. The Pope arrived in Mexico, Supreme Court Justice Antonin Scalia was killed, and the Grand Mosque Caliphate connected with the Russian Patriarch Kirill to receive *Instructions given to Muhammad* to process the Ark of Gabriel delivered to the Holy Trinity church in Antarctica by a Russian navel fleet! Top that! At their Joint Declaration in Havana Pope Francis and Patriarch Kirill somehow prepared the migration of World elites to settle in New Zealand. Amid Obama and bigwig visits our **Melt** finds a masonry grid buried in Antarctica later dug up to prepare convincing evidence, not that the aliens are coming, but that they are here. ***Autopsy of Scalia's Hat*** as a footnote to *Melt* describes the fairy tale surroundings of Justice Scalia's death as somehow a propitiation for both Trump and the Pope. We have clearly left the land of the knowable.

Thanks and acknowledgments to Rachael Kendall of *Sein und Werden*, Russell Streur of *Camel Saloon Gallery* and Doc Sigerson of *Red Fez*, for even though that *Fez* is now offline and defunct, it first published these. Since a version of *Opiomes* appeared at *Eyeshot*, thanks also to Lee Klein. Aspects of A Tale of Two Towers appeared in *Emanations: When a Planet Was a Planet*.

Isaiah in America, the Faerie Queene Cometh

"I know that there is only the smallest measure of inspiration that can be taken from this devastation, but there is a passage in the Bible from Isaiah that I think speaks to all of us at times like this, 'the bricks have fallen down, but we will rebuild with dressed stone: the sycamore figs have been felled, but we will replace them with cedars.' That is what we will do" (Tom Daschle, 9/12, 2001).

"I believe one of the first things we should commit to – with federal help that underscores our nation's purpose – is to rebuild the towers of the World Trade Center and show the world we are not afraid – *we are defiant*." [17]   (September 12, 2001, Senator John Kerry, US Senate).

Some say it is because *sheol* had to expand they put up new towers from "a great depopulation in the midst of the land" (*Isaiah* 6.12). Alcohol and drug use doubled the work. Datura production increased. Great applause came from the Depopulate the Earth movement and Margaret Sanger selling used body parts. But the first proof that America was in the Bible came when bats were being cast into idols, and then when the fly and the bee were summoned into camp from all "the holes of the rocks and upon all thorns to **settle *upon all bushes***" (Isaiah 7.19). Consider that the flies had already encamped the Bushes before that better fly, Assyria and its modern counterpart, got into America with Obama.

Why apocalypse? Because there is so no self parody in public life American leaders connected America and Israel. It isn't only Tom Daschle, Senate Majority Leader who boggles the mind. He was just the first. Speaking for "both parties," "both houses" and all "212 years" he introduced the joint resolution of House and Senate. Edwards, Giuliani, Pataki, Obama, Kerry made so what the puritans and evangelicals had long before.

Nobody connected Jerusalem, Washington **and** New York (first inaugural of George Washington in 1789) with Isaiah and 9/11 until Daschle. These comparisons were not the comfort legislators thought. Isaiah says, "the princes are rebellious and companions of thieves, where everyone loves bribes" (1.23), that the news media "are soothsayers like the Philistines" (2.6), that the American economy "full of silver and gold, has no end of treasure" (2.7), is a "land is full of idols" (2.8). It is Anthony Weiner in the yard, so to speak. The full quote reads: "mankind become degenerate as the great man debased himself" (2.9), "in the pride and haughtiness of heart."

So when "the bricks are fallen down, but we will build with dressed stone: the sycamore figs are cut, but we will replace them with cedars, adversaries shall be set up against them, enemies joined together; the Syrians before, the Philistines behind; and they shall swallow them with open mouth." (*Isaiah* 9.10). That's the context of Daschle's "blessing," two lines out of many disasters for America.

Daschling The House of Pride.

"In the pride and haughtiness of heart,"
Edmund Spenser said:

> "Some frounce their curled Hair in courtly guise,
> Some pranke their Ruffes, and others trimly dight
> Their gay Attire: each others greater Pride does spight.

> His drunken Corse he scarce upholden can;
> In Shape and Life, more like a Monster than a Man. (FQ, iv)

Then Daschle (again):

"I know that there is only the smallest measure of inspiration that can be taken from this devastation. But there is a passage in the Bible from Isaiah that I think speaks to us all at times like this.

'The bricks have fallen down but we will rebuild with dressed stone; the fig trees have been felled but we will replace them with cedars.'

"That is what we will do. We will rebuild and we will recover, the people of America will stand strong together because the people of America have always stood together. And those of us privileged to serve this great nation will stand with you. God bless the people of America." here.

Also gain, the complete text of Isaiah says:

"All that say in the pride and haughtiness of heart,
the bricks are fallen down, but we will build with dressed stone:
the sycamore figs are cut, but we will replace them with cedars,
shall have adversaries set up against them
enemies joined together; the Syrians before, the Philistines behind;
and they shall swallow them with open mouth." (Isaiah 9.10)

Sycamore root

Is anybody home in Daschle's head? When hewn stone and cedar replace bricks and sycamore that provoke alliances against them, fantasy turns real, like they said. Daschle's words come true after he says them. The Sycamore at Ground Zero that sheltered St Paul's Chapel, causing it to survive with hardly a window broken, those roots, bronzed, and its stump memorialized on the spot, were replaced by a cedar! The empty place of the Sycamore has been filled.

But further, consider that the **first American Capitol** was four blocks from Ground Zero, seeming to indicate that the fall of the towers was a symbolic attack on the founding of the Republic itself. How far were the "symbols and structures of our economic and military strength" compromised?

The Syrians! Keep reading, **if you wrote this in a Greek play it would sound contrived.** America can beat Russia, China, Iran, Iraq, al Qaeda, ISIS, but God? America has to beat God. A large pine, cousin of the cedar, was lowered into the empty hole with the destiny of the words.

Spider at Guggenheim Bilbao

"I believe one of the first things we should commit to – with federal help that underscores our nation's purpose – is to rebuild the towers of the World Trade Center and show the world we are not afraid – *we are defiant*. John Kerry, US Senate, September 12, 2001.

Jack Ryan, John Kerry, Kevin Costner will prevent the apocalypse! What happened to the bricks? Right! The Governor of New York ordered a 20 ton block of granite quarried from the Adirondacks to be the new cornerstone at Ground Zero. A gratuitous symbol, completely unnecessary, just PR and puffery, boasting like John Kerry saying we will **show the world we are not afraid** – *we are defiant.* Who is there to defy anyway, for you can only defy a power greater than you, and surely he's not of Al-Qaeda? What's wrong with this hewn, dressed stone? Answer, in Israel anyway (and now of course America is like Israel), cutting and polishing pollutes the stone, imparts pride and haughtiness of heart,

> If you make a stone altar
> don't make it of hewn stone
> any tool that touches it pollutes it
> (*Exodus* 20:25).

These particulars of pride can be explored by analogy. To be sure the first course of government is denial and ridicule that such "coincidences" exist. If they do exist they are happenstance, not collateral damage. Collateral damage is saved for the effects of their own drones. No government drones have yet been mounted against the harbinger.

> Huge Routs of People did about them band,
> Shouting for Joy; and still before their way
> A foggy Mist had covered all the Land;
> And underneath their Feet, all scattered lay
> Dead Skulls and Bones of Men, whose Life had gone astray.
> (*FQ* I.4.xxxvi)

Government is all powerful to obscure. Look for one approach to be that Isaiah is anti-gay for his remarks against Sodom, and anti-woman, for those tinkling feet **of the daughters of Zion whose secret parts are bared**. But there is no avoiding the obvious, Isaiah is the last place America would ever want to be. Any sequence of the history of Israel tells you that. The trouble is, can you take the words back?

Will the present speaker of the house and the senate leader renounce the cedar and hewn stone? It might do some good to take back a lot of former oaths. But if America *is* a symbolic Israel expect to have the hedge taken away (*Isaiah* 5.5), for it to be laid waste (5.6) (and directly related to the 9.10 curse), "swallowed with open mouth." "Hell is enlarged, opens without measure. Their glory descends into it" (5.14).

Quibblers may disallow the sycamore/cedar, brick/hewn stone analogy to say that the Isaiah tree was not a true sycamore like the one in New York, and that anyway Pataki's foundation stone was not in the end used by the builders of Freedom Tower. Not used. But the further you dig into the botany the stronger the parallels get. The greater prophecy had already said,

"in the Last Days (Isaiah 2.2)...every one that is proud and lofty, every one lifted up shall be brought low; the cedars of Lebanon...and every high tower...the loftiness of man shall be bowed down...the idols utterly abolished" (2.12-18).

Isaiah Line by Line. Laptop Fickle Freaks. Not to go line by line, the fundamental premise of Isaiah's judgment repeats over and over that human pride shall be humbled (Isaiah 2.11), the lofty

shall be bowed down (Isaiah 2.17), and that their boldness proves
their character (Isaiah 3.9). Doubled down!

They are as proud as Sodom of themselves, "they hide it not,"
meaning they have no shame. The crack about Sodom doesn't
have the sting for the current U. S. that it did for Isaiah, who took
Sodom as an opposite case from Jonah's Nineveh, which changed
its ways. Every day in America, the top is down, the bottom up,
Sodom, porn, abortion join particular idols made with hands,
iPods, iPhones, laptops, toggle bunnies and video games to average
66 hours of screen time a week. Isaiah has them casting their (idol)
laptops to bats and moles (Isaiah 2.20). Reception might be poor
in the clefts and tops of ragged rocks where they hide (Isaiah 2.21),
or maybe they have left their idols behind in the scramble to
survive at the tops of apartment buildings.

> A stately Palace built of squared Brick,
> Which cunningly was without Mortar laid,
> Whose Walls were high, but nothing strong, nor thick;
> And golden Foil all over them displaid;
> That purest Sky with Brightness they dismaid:
> High lifted up were many lofty Towers,
> (FQ I, iv, 4)

> That every Breath of Heaven shaked it;
> And all the hinder parts, that few could spy,
> Were ruinous and old, but painted cunningly.
> (iv, 50)

When the stay and staff of Isaiah's prophecy are moved and helter
skelter myth politic runs along with shortages of bread and water
(*Isaiah* 3.1), the boundaries go down. People disdain their unseen

protections of the boundary hedge for their connectedness with each other in the social, neural connectome!, which outcome is the demolition of leadership (3.2-5). Everybody's humanity is flouted. The judge, prophet, elder, lawyer, artist and speaker are removed. Shouted down by hordes, one of a hundred. My brother, nobody special, wouldn't even rule in their place, says Isaiah. "Don't vote for me," he says (*Isaiah* 3.7), "who wants to rule ruin?" So they get some children, "children are their tyrants" (3.12), the everlastingly puerile of heart and mind who train at our club, frat boys in their 60s with the moles, bats, cedars, towers, children, Sodom, pride and idols: Tom Daschle speaketh! Was this a mousetrap dead fall to catch the prey engineered in advance by Al-Qaeda or was it a lucky strike like the cigarette? It gets worse. Is it God? A symbolic strike to the heart, as Daschle so kindly says. He didn't realize George Washington's Inaugural and Federal Hall, first American Capital were four blocks from Ground Zero, in **"the heart of the American community and the symbols and structures."** Didn't know it would be 14 buildings in all.

None of this gets mentioned without the American senators bringing it up! It is done more than once, John Edwards did it, and all Presidents echo the *bigger better* theme. In chapter eight, in a series of ominous predictions, Isaiah says he and his children are signs and wonders. The greater signs come in **a series of progressions**, small warnings followed by large. The principle is that the people who resist the rising of the soft waters of Shiloh in Rezin and Remaliah will be swept up to their necks by the floods of the king of Assyria. They need to heed the first warning, but don't, so the second comes. Floods have no power themselves except to provoke change. And by implication after the second comes a third, and pretty soon America's not in the Bible again. It is washed away. To resist is to make them worse. Likewise in

Isaiah 9, "at first He lightly afflicted that land of Zebulon and the land of Naphtali, but at last **he will deal hard by the way of the sea**" (Isaiah9.1). There go the coasts.

These progressions continue their reversals, "associate yourselves and you will be broken...gird yourselves and be broken...take counsel and come to nothing...speak a word and it will be defeated (Isaiah 8.9,10). There is profit in alliances, "let Him be your fear" (Isaiah 8.13), but help is not found in the usual wisdom of diviners (Isaiah 8.19). All avenues fail, "the living should not inquire of the dead." When the Assyrian flood comes, the conquered will be hungry, get angry and curse their king president and his senate deities. Instead of looking "upward for help" they "look to earth...and are driven into darkness" (Isaiah 8.21-22). This is the pattern of events the American Speaker invokes, one warning unheeded, followed by a worse. Shiloh, Assyrian flood, forced march to Babylon. By no means believe everything your government does for your security, right up until the series of big surprises to come. They want to get their towers back up. Government leaders, corporate NGOs, selected Scientology and religious groups have a minimum of 1500 underground sites (UG) worldwide connected by mag-lev trains via the mo-hole in which to hide. But even though it is the American leaders who invoke this "blessing," Isaiah says it is the "people" (8.6) who refuse the soft waters of Shiloh. **Aren't the people given points off in** their spoiling because of mind control manipulation by corporate governments and military? Sorry, all are in it together. That's why if the people spoke up now they would feel less a foolish victim. Join the revolution against Monsanto?

The basic harbinger info of J. Cahn has had multiple shares of every sort. He says members of Congress have visited the sites with him and prayed. What did they pray for anyway, the prevention of disaster brought on by arrogance? Nobody wins against the force of entertainment patriotism. When JayZ, Charlie Rose, and all the monarched up movie stars and entertainment figures plead for the government to save us, deliver us from evil, know that government has replaced the larger thing that its senate defies. Paul Anka says when he was with the Rat Pack in Vegas, with Sinatra, Martin, Sammy Davis Jr. etc., they all knew they worked for the bosses of organized crime, but that didn't make them criminal, he says, and they were all right as long as they stayed in their place. Organized crime ran all the big clubs, networks, film studios, publishers. If you wanted to go along you got along. Spense's Envy serves as an analogy to government.

> Between his cankered Teeth a venomous Toad,
> That all the Poison ran about his Jaw;
> But inwardly he chewed his own Maw
> At Neighbor's Wealth, that made him ever sad;
> *(FQ,* I, 4, 30)

For each dissent there are a hundred, a thousand shills who psychoanalyze motive and twist fact. The thing is, something like Isaiah 9.10 unmasks the arrogance and its naked control. It is as if government were a giant colossi, a sumu wrestler big as a building, naked, ponderous. If you don't like the Vegas Crime boss analogy for D.C./NY, try Monsanto, which has the entire government in its pocket to convince the Europeans not to ban GMO products. All the while they are saving your life they are killing you. You can believe the entertainment news and entrainment education. Even if disbelief is manipulated.

House of Pride

This allegory of the Pride of Congress has two natures, moral-religious and national-political, particularly concerning Lucifera and the procession of the seven deadly sins (*FQ*, I, Cantos iv, v). Lucifera is not far from the daughter of Zion with her "hinder parts painted cunningly." Pride is an illusion with no basis in reality like Chaucer's *House of Fame* that has the names of great men inscribed on the north wall and their destruction on the south. The leprosy (*Isaiah* 3.17) of the Daughters and their bared secret parts is like the escapees of the House by the side of the road "in most wretched case." Literature is good for something, to talk besides the unmentionable, which Spenser voluminously did with the Tudors. The House of Pride is ready to crumble at any moment, for "every breath of heaven shaked it (iv, 5. 7). The inhabitants are infinite sorts of people, the best of the diversity of hell no doubt, a nation diverse as its own pride. The lords and ladies, the government await Queen Lucifera but are only props to her appearance. There is a lot of parody. She brooks no rivals. To cast our male presidents into the roles they play as maiden queens does not deny the strict controls behind them. Lucifera is the false light of pride whose carriage is puffed by the seven deadly sins. Gluttony has been surrendered along with pride, and lechery, envy, wrath.

> His ruffin raiment all was staind with blood,
> Which he had spilt, and all to rags yrent (FQ, iv. 34. 1-2)

What exactly are our seven deadly sins? Just to show this is not a prophecy of the Obama age, after the six unholy pairs have passed in review, we see Satan the lackey, riding on the wagon beam, lashing the beasts onward. They pass through the mass of people, and through a "foggy mist' that covers the land before they find the "fresh flowering fields' and the "solace of the open air." The procession tramples over the skulls and bones of those who had previously come this way, "whose life had gone astray." Maybe Spenser was quoting Isaiah like Daschle (5.18):

> Woe unto them that draw iniquity with cords
> of vanity, and sin as it were with a cart rope.

Ben Franklin

In the dungeons of the burning lake gods by the seaside lie. In the palace the bodies of thousands beside themselves with pride could never leave this House (Sparknotes), like the basement excavations at the Ben Franklin House when Franklin lived in London, boasted as the only remaining Franklin Home where Franklin lived 1757-75. Most of the bones, 200 years old, dissected, sawn and cut, one skull drilled with several holes, says Paul Knapman, the Westminster Coroner who saw in "a pit in a windowless basement where sticking out of the dirt floor, a human thigh bone." The Franklin House was only trying to spruce the place up when they discovered this. Animal remains were found as well. Cover up the bones of Pride. The true and false are nearly interchanged. Una takes Archimago to be Redcross, Redcross takes Duessa to be Una. Should we apply this technique to American government, Daschle takes America to be Israel. Google *The Harbinger* of 9/11 and get all the elaborate explanations of Isaiah 9.10. Then Google Revelation 9/11. How did America finally get in the Bible? It wasn't there before. Russia, China and Egypt were, but if the greatest power on earth wasn't in the Bible, in the last days it was dropped smack into chapter nine of Isaiah. One caution, chapters two to fourteen of Isaiah are called the **Mother of all Threatening**s as Edward Young says. When Israel in Isaiah took every counsel of its own advising, which all failed, and continued

doing so, until finally, in chapter fourteen, guess who comes?
"How art thou fallen thou son of the morning?"

Cahn says 9/11 was "the first" warning, in concert with Isaiah 9.1,
"*at first* He lightly afflicted." The sequencing repeats the
progression of Shiloh to the Assyrian flood. There are implicit
middle terms in this. How many warnings before "*at the last* He
will deal hard" (9.1)? The first trigger event begins a sequence of
increasing scale, followed by a second, inferential, the financial
meltdown seven years to the week after 9/11. The point however
is that from the two a third and on are projected until "the last."
This assumes the warnings are not taken, behavior is unchanged, in
fact it gets worse. One way it gets worse is that as the public, I
mean the mass mind, becomes aware of warnings, the forces that
rule bring out their drones to destroy awareness. Thus of the third
event, putatively set for *September 2015*, only the fool will speak,
not for fear of being wrong, but for being marked for certain
destruction by the drones. These will ridicule, psychoanalyze,
grammatically deconstruct, defame, exaggerate to destroy, utterly
misrepresent the event and its revelator. When however the event
comes to pass, the drones will extinct the memory in the popular
mass mind. Do these forces really have the power to so manipulate
public awareness and memory of the past? You with your 66 hours
of screen time a week ask. It is a fiat accompli. Too bad America
doesn't believe in Yahweh, especially when its leaders so
sagaciously flaunt His counsel. You say you believe, but help thou
my unbelief if you swallow entertainment patriotism, terrorists
threats as real, if you unquestioningly swallow the entertainment
fugues giving you the peace sign, the devil sign, aping Horus and
every jujube of Babylon. I guess you think this song is about you,
don't you?

America summons all the threats but none of the blessings. These first fourteen chapters of Isaiah are filled with both. It is almost always saying His hand is stretched out still, but it's not the hand of a beggar on the freeway, it's the hand of help to pull you out of where the waters get up your neck. No we can't have that! America can stand on its own two feet. Two feet, four feet, six feet and holler, our SWAT teams will bring the new order! How else talk. First warning was the Towers. Second warning the financial meltdown close to exactly seven years later, says J. Cahn. Humbled. Humbled. (5.15). Third warning the blood moons and cardinal cross? Isaiah keeps saying that sheol has gotten a lot bigger from the influx (5.14). Woe unto them that call evil good (5.20), murder a woman's right, start there with Moloch. You better take a drink before we go (5.22). Man if you read 5.27-30 you might weep from the whirlwind wheels, what soothsayers call weather changes, lions, lions, roar roaring sea, darkness!

That was the year king Uzziah died and Isaiah saw the posts of the door move at the voice (6.4). That was when he began his ministry of telling "this people in hearing you listen but you will not understand" (6.9). They had a bad case of Fat Heart (6.10). Say all that to say this, sheol had to expand, put up new towers since there was then "a great depopulation in the midst of the land" (6.12). Oh hell yes Daschle bring us into the Bible. We will double the alcohol and drug supply. Work continues on all fronts to increase datura production. The biggest applause is from Depopulate the 90% movement. Margaret Sanger and well, you don't want to know who. There are good shows on tonight. Let's get a cappuccino. First he had them casting their idols to bats, splendid, and moles, don't forget the moles, but now he summons the fly and the bee to camp in all "the holes of the rocks and upon all thorns and upon all bushes" (7.19). Further proof America is in the Bible.

The flies have already encamped upon the Bushes. Thing is, these flies are Assyrians, so we have to come up with the modern counterpart to really get America back out of the Bible.

> Young Knight, whatever that dost Arms profess,
> And through long Labors huntest after Fame,
> Beware of Fraud, beware of Fickleness,
> In Choice and Change of thy dear loved Dame;
> Lest thou of her believe too lightly blame,
> And rash misweening do thy Heart remove;
> For unto Knight there is no greater Shame,
> Than Lightness and Inconstancy in Love;
> That doth this Red-cross Knight's ensample plainly prove. here

To show how vain the groove in the record that the apocalypse is coming, this is not Paul Revere's call to arms and flight, or an attempt to score readership in China and Ukraine. So many duds, so little time. I bring the Harbinger to the *Faerie Queene*. That should be obscure enough. Edmund Spenser got in trouble predicting Mary Queen of Scots was a type of the Great Whore of Babylon (Duessa). All England was a backdrop of his myth of King Arthur, Rome, the Bible and Babylon. Can it go further, that America is a backdrop for the new world order anti-messiah? It depends on commerce, beauty, truth and art. Buying and selling souls. I quote Dame Edith on this, "who buys, who buys, come lay your pence upon my staring lidless eyes."

Revelation 18 is a summation of this commerce of preoccupied patriarchs and prophets buying and selling favor, religion, blood, children, women, goods and service. Add in the 20 centuries succeeding and the stars of commerce will do anything to serve their need, get down on all fours and moo like a cow. *When the stars threw their spears*, when the stars are shaken and fall like figs, who had a good run, those trumpets angels blow at earth's imagined corners unloose the long awaited judgment on commerce. As such it's time to shop for a hole, it's time to bring the *Faerie Queene* to explain 9/11. It will get stranger. It's important to hedge one's bets, more Delphic than the moon, in case of another Delphic dud.

joint resolution

A Tale of Two Towers

"However we explain the phenomenon, it forces on our minds a truth which the incurably evolutionary or

*developmental character of modern thought is always urging us to forget. What is vital and healthy does not necessarily survive. Higher organisms are often conquered by lower ones...an art, a whole civilization, may at any time slip through **mens' fingers** in a very few years and be gone beyond recovery. IF WE ARE ALIVE WHEN SUCH A THING IS HAPPENING WE SHALL HARDLY NOTICE IT UNTIL TOO LATE; AND IT IS MOST UNLIKELY THAT WE SHALL KNOW ITS CAUSES."*

C. S. Lewis, *Sixteenth Century*, 113.

A representative body implicates a nation. September 12, 2001, Tom Daschle, Senate Majority Leader, introduced a <u>joint resolution</u> condemning the attacks, emphasizing that he spoke for all, both houses and parties. He linked his remarks to the founding of the Republic. The site of the first American capitol and inauguration of George Washington in 1789 was four blocks from Ground Zero. Daschle did not know how far the "symbols and structures of our economic and military strength" were compromised. He did not know that when he linked America with ancient Israel in the prophecy of Isaiah that instead of "God bless the people of America" he was delivering a curse.

"It is with pain, sorrow, anger and resolve that I stand before this Senate, assembled for **212 years** of the strength of our democracy and say that America will emerge from this tragedy as we have emerged from all adversity, united and strong. The America in which we woke today is far different from the one in which we woke yesterday. This morning as our rescue workers and medical personnel continue their heroic work we begin to truly understand **the enormity** of what happened. My heart aches for the people of New York, our men and women serving at the Pentagon, the passengers and crew of the four hijacked aircraft and for their families and friends. These attacks were an assault on our people and on our freedom. They aimed at **the heart of the American community and the symbols and structures of our economic and military** strength. As an American, as an elected representative I am outraged, as a husband, as a father I am pained beyond words. Last night we sent a message to the world that even in the face of such cowardly and heinous acts the doors of democracy will not close. **This joint resolution** we lay down today condemns yesterday's attacks, expresses our sympathy for the victims and our support for the president as our commander in chief. The world should know that the **members of both parties** in both houses stand united in this. The full resources of our government will be brought to bear in aiding the search and rescue and in hunting down those responsible and those who may have aided or harbored them. Nothing, nothing can replace the losses of those that have suffered."

"I know that there is only the smallest measure of inspiration that can be taken from this devastation. But there is a passage in the Bible from Isaiah that I think speaks to us all at times like this. **'The bricks have fallen down but we will rebuild with dressed stone; the fig trees have been felled but we will replace them with cedars.'** That is what we will do. We will rebuild and we will recover, the people of America will stand strong together because the people of America have always stood together. And those of us privileged to serve this great nation will stand with you. God bless the people of America." <u>here</u>

Isaiah words were spoken in the moment of the Assyrian assault. When Jerusalem's buildings and towers fell and its trees were cut it vowed to rebuild better, stronger that before. How exactly this spells out in America's coming years, through the market meltdown that came seven years later, and what would come in seven more years at 2015 is left to be surmised, except J Cahn has laid it out.

The first to suggest Isaiah the biblical prophet predicts 9/11 is the senate majority leader after 9/11, Tom Daschle, but the commissions that implemented the site restoration of Ground Zero, were the ones who put in the hewn stone, and lowered the cedar into the sycamore's hole. all different agencies in this case, but the overall attitude of the restoration was shared from Bush to Obama, who recently, wrote on the beam, "We remember We rebuild We come back stronger." That's when giant boots began to tramp back and forth across the country making holes and shallows and swamps and thumps ... IF WE ARE ALIVE WHEN SUCH A THING IS HAPPENING but no one could see above the tops. WE SHALL HARDLY NOTICE IT UNTIL TOO LATE; AND IT IS MOST UNLIKELY THAT WE SHALL KNOW ITS CAUSES…" "Depressions left by their feet in the park drowned the little dogs." Now you know what they are.

The kryptonite of Israel was the attitude that it would *defy* its enemy, because the defiance was really against Yahweh. Isaiah makes this clear. He shouts Isaiah 9.10 at them, says that they might say they will replace the bricks with hewn stone, the sycamore's with cedar and built ever stronger and bigger, but they won't. Hewn stone is celebrated as being stronger than the hand made brick, and cedar than sycamore, stick right up in the face they do. But Daschle speaks a curse against America when he speaks Isaiah's words. They were not a blessing, not a defense. So why does Daschle so potently identify America with Israel in its moment of Assyrian terror? Because he has a tin ear. That this tin ear keeps ticking and echoing. NY boasts it will cut a 20 ton piece of stone from the Adirondacks to use as a new cornerstone for the new Freedom Tower, later rejected. The Sycamore tree at Ground Zero that sheltered the miracle chapel is replaced by a "cedar,' a cousin pine tree. The new tower is bigger than before, raised to boasts, shaking fists, threats bravado and resolve, even to the point of continued use of language, the word defy. This puts America front and center into the bible of Isaiah 9. 10. Chapter and verse, that's where America is in the Bible. Who do they defy, al queda/ Ridiculous. you only defy some thing greater than yourself, not less. But no more than Ancient Israel does America know what it is doing when it shakes its fist. I have good news and bad, the Cahn's harbingers only partly apply, however the part that does is worse than he lets on for Tom Daschle's senate floor if we look earlier in *Isaiah* where there is more about the cedar and the stone and fist.

"For the day of Yahweh of hosts shall be upon every one that is proud and lofty, and upon every one that is lifted up and he shall be brought low. And upon all the cedars of Lebanon that are high and lifted up...and upon every high tower...and the loftiness of man shall be bowed down...and the idols He shall utterly abolish."

Moreover the conditions of that day are set forth for Yah-Yahweh shall "take away from Jerusalem and from Judah the stay and the staff" (3.1), that is to say, the guard, the protection, the covering extended over the righteous nation from the many that opposed it. In the destruction that follows more is taken away: "the mighty man, the warrior, judge, prophet, the prudent, the elder, the captain, the honorable, the counselor, the artist, the orator" are replaced by children: "I will give children for the princes...and the child shall behave himself proudly against the elder and the base against the honorable. The rule of law fails."

Isaiah won't stop (9). The boldness of the faces witness against them and they declare their sin as Sodom, they hide it not. That tears it for the modern American confidant of Sodom, but Isaiah doesn't care for "they have done evil unto themselves." When he says "children are their tyrants" he means their leadership is puerile and meaningless. Check the pols, are there any adults in Washington? But it gets worse. They "lay bare their secret parts" (4.17). This is not just Olympia underwear, but secret texts, mistresses, deals, leaks on and on. so that we will never be done with the effects of Isaiah before 9.10. This is called the Day of the Lord, the End times, the Last Days and America just got there in time Young says anarchy follows from poor govt I.144, but the full picture in the 9 chapters is filled out with "the mother of all threatenings 347 and the end result, "they shall eat every man of the flesh of his own arm." It's time to break out the stars and stripes. Given the imperfect nature of our knowledge it may be more important to understand how we rationalize away what we do know rather than look for more knowing. So to understand Isaiah and 9/11, take a substitute 3 parallel, **James Laughlin and** 9/11

Poet Ezra Pound told James Laughlin, founder and publisher of New Directions Press, "you're never going to be any good as a poet." But **Nobody** said he was a prophet well maybe poet Wendell Berry, for Laughlin's "Above the City" of 1946 *accidently* predicts the fall of the Twin Towers of 2001.

Various claims predicting 9/11 told what remote view psychic spies knew, what Nostradamus knew, what the Feds knew, CIA knew. You can search "who knew 9/11," but blind Olympus and the Oedipus kings of Greece prove that seeing doesn't see. Poets aren't always prophetic even *after* the event. Cortez, not Balboa, discovered the Pacific in Keats! Nassim Nicholas Taleb says he did not predict 9/11, even if he did. Published a week before 9/11 he said there was a possibility that a plane would crash into an office building. But that's nothing beside McLaughlin's poem, and McLaughlin is nothing beside the Harbinger that entrance America into the bible at 9/11.

If the rational denies the literal what happens to the Tower guy? Explained away: "the details are wrong. It wasn't the *18th floor*. The South Tower was hit above the 86th floor, the North Tower above the 96th. It wasn't *Saturday morning*, it was Tuesday. And the "bomber" was really an airliner, two of them. And anyway World Trade Center didn't exist in 1946. It opened in 1970. Sure there are two towers in Laughlin's poem, Salmon Tower and Empire State, but they're not "the twin towers." Even if they are called "two paragons of progress," Laughlin's poem is literally a poetic commentary on an actual such collision of a B-25 bomber that crashed into the 79th floor of the Empire State Building 28 July 1945. It can almost be seen live: "Bomber Hits Skyscraper in Heavy Fog."

A flat reportorial conversational style draws the reader in confidence. The 58 story Salmon Tower, immediate precursor to the Empire State Building of 102 stories, the tallest building in New York City prior to the North Tower of the World Trade Center of 1972, is hit by a plane. The significance is not in the details but in their embellishment. It is Saturday morning in the poem. They are working late, or early in a matter of fact tone, "finishing up some late invoices" in another office building. The writer sees a plane, which he calls a bomber because it is a bomber in the news. Like an apparition it "roars through the mist" and crashes as if by implication into the Empire State. Flames pour from the windows after the explosion. The "two paragons of progress," either the airplane and the building, or by extension the two buildings, perform before our eyes their true relationship," that is, they fall.

Above the City

You know our office on the 18th
floor of the Salmon Tower looks
right out on the

Empire State and it just happened
we were there finishing up some
late invoices on

a new book that Saturday morning
when a bomber roared through the
mist and crashed

flames poured from the windows
into the drifting clouds and sirens
screamed down in

the streets below it was unearthly
but you know the strangest thing
we realized that

none of us were much surprised be-

cause we'd always known that those
two paragons of

progress sooner or later would perform before our eyes this demon-
stration of their
true relationship.

It's almost as if alternate futures revealed themselves continually but only sometimes were recognized. Prophetic facts! Either that or the 1946 crash and the 2001 act were random events, but it is easier to believe the conspirators knew of the previous crash and copied it than that the two events are unconnected as though facts were prophetic in themselves, as if every news account were capable of bearing future analogues to random events, black swans, a prophetic journalism of the future that history does or doesn't repeat.

The poet Wendell Berry, who doubts the McLaughlin prophet, stands in for government doubters of the prophet events of Ground Zero in Isaiah. "It is tempting to call this poem "prophetic." But it is only so in the sense that it is insightful; it perceives the implicit contradiction between tall buildings and airplanes. This contradiction was readily apparent also to the terrorists of September 11, but evidently invisible within the mist of technological euphoria that had surrounded the great innovators and decision makers" (*Citizenship Papers*, 2003, Berry, 98).

Berry makes it a moral lesson on blindness, as if poets are better at morality than Keats at history. Berry makes the text "the results of great decisions not adequately informed" (99). In addition to tall buildings he fears for nuclear power plants and a food supply system threatened with bioterrorism as much as others might fear the fall of the dollar, unemployment and the housing market. He calls it a failure of the "rational mind."

But the problem of predicted events is how far ahead they occur. Prediction to be valuable has to fall in a window of usefulness. Knowing a rise in the price of gold, the market up or down, depression, war are only valuable in a lifetime. These are all things pundits predict, but not assassinations, floods, earthquakes. Those are for prophets. In the medieval time they prophesied by the three Ds, death, decay, disease. If Laughlin's 1946 prophetic journalism predates its historical fulfillment and he and we don't know he's doing it, what good is it?

But there is more than one point of comparison with the twin towers. There are three direct correlations along with the literal towers in the poem, Salmon Tower and Empire State, furthered by their being called "two paragons," that make the insight. It isn't just an airplane, it's "*a bomber*." And when it strikes the Empire State Building in the poem, "*flames poured from the windows*," exactly what happened at the explosion of the fuel tanks. Likewise "*sirens screamed down in the streets below*," closely resembling the call in which 341 firefighters died, along with the massive police and EMS response: All of this can come under eventualities that occur when "the great innovators and decision makers build huge airplanes whose loads of fuel make them, in effect, flying bombs. And they build the World Trade Center, forgetting apparently the B-25 bomber that crashed into the seventy-ninth floor of the Empire State Building in 1945. And then on September 11, 2001 some enemies-of a kind we well knew we had and evidently had decided to ignore-captured two huge airplanes and flew them, as bombs, into the two towers of the World Trade

Center. In retrospect, we may doubt that those shaping decisions were properly informed, just as we may doubt that the expansive "intelligence" that is supposed to foresee and prevent such disasters is sufficiently intelligent" (Berry, 97).When Berry is do we don't feel so bad, as though it's all been a mistake that **Nobody** could have foreseen, and certainly there is no suggestion that it is a divine mousetrap.

Not all news accounts are prophetic as a B-25 bomber awaiting time and place, but who thinks ahead and changes their behavior

on the basis of a past event? **Nobody**! Right again. Instead they wait for the event to happen and react, but not ahead of time. Thus, to further Berry's rationalisms, it seems inevitable that in millenniums ahead the tale of two towers will be compared to myth, taken as allegory and doubted as fact. Reduced to interpretation, there may be little difference between news accounts and archeological speculations of ziggurats on Babylon's plain, excavations of Troy VIIA and the Fall of Babel, a "story possibly… inspired by the fall of the famous temple-tower of Etemenanki." The towers will symbolize Ilium and the dissolution of the Ring. New York, Troy-Babel, will show the limit of reason. Beowulf, Faustus, Milton, Blake, imprisoned in the stone where Merlin lay as a symbol of the brain, will, with venetian blinds, vinyl chairs and the prescience of technology show poets as the unacknowledged journalists of the world.

These events are symbolic before the fact and after, explained as either natural causes or symbolic, whether 3000 or 60 years separate the two, the Judgment of nations, kings, Greek fate, where blinded fury strikes with the anointed spear Lycidas or Oedipus, who can do nothing but be driven by hubris to this fate, there kings make mistakes because of good intent or pride and have their eyes put out, like King Zedekiah, last king of Judah,   or dreams and omens vex the court of the king Arthur and the courts of a nation. We insist two different things. When for entertainment we revel in our paradox, *te deum deus ex machina* should these not dare to appear in current events! Government, industry, church, academia and all the world powers oppose this understanding. There can be no such thing as fate, destiny or judgment, judgment for sin, hamartia, hubris overreaching. Fate is not a topic of journalism but of literature.

As if fate put into current events causes taken as hysteria, as if the thoughts of madmen were broadcast over the news. Except the thoughts of millions of madmen *are* broadcast over all the self generated media to then be reported by the mainstream reality. Mainstream Reality is a special brand of hysteria where the more ignorant and partisan the louder and more extreme the voice. This passes for public discourse. Against this backdrop fate hand out omens.

Presidents and anarchitects of drone strikes should appreciate the nuance. It's as if a missile were launched on the other ide of the world to strike at the symbolic heart of the American government, which depending on the day, would be either its duly constituted right or commercial power. Taking the case, the missiles airpliances stuck unknowing, which just happened to be this first inaugural spot. Call it collateral damage. When American drones do this in paristand or Afganistan it is winked at and called the fog of war, likewise when the Federal Hall was awash in ash it was dismissed and the promise was to **rebuild bigger** and stronger, so as not to seem to have been defeated.

But journalism catches up to lit as if Trayvon Martin were "a sacrifice for all of us." Which hysteria, Victor Cruz of the Giants said, "Zimmerman doesn't last a year til the hood catches up to him." Roddy White of the Falcons, "them jurors should go home tonight and kill themselves for letting a grown man get away with killing a kid." In those years abortion had already become an act of heroism for human rights, pornography raising the banner of free speech, and gay marriage the liberation of hope.

No govt ever thought it did anything wrong. Governments to do not believe in the judgement of God on them, they believe in their judgement upon their enemies. So even if there were omissions and failures in Behghazi or 9/11… no symbolic event is seen as natural, it is explained away as effectively as Wendell Berry does McLaughlin.

When Jerry Falwell seemed to say the day after that 9/11 was the judgment of God people went as nuts as when Michelle Bachmann repeated it a decade later and added Benghazi of 9/11/12 to the list. Of course Rabbi Cahn would add the stock crash of 9/16 2008 to

the list. None of these events produced regret in the pundits or the government, just the opposite. To them the judgment of God was a right wing plot. *Why then do the nations so furiously rage together, the people imagine a vain thing?*

It was always a scandal that <u>America was not in the Bible</u>. Books and even CIA sermons written about it could find no mention prophetically that America participated in the end times of *Revelations*. This was troubling to Americans because after two thousand the end times were practically the only topic of conversation. Much comfort was gained then when America, we should call it the United States, found a way to get in the Bible. Indeed Tom Dashel did it the day after 9/11, which was anyway a day much prophecied, even if the prophecies were denied. I don't mean Nostradamus, but New Directions publisher McLaughlins planes fling in the buildings in 1948, but after the event, the next day, 9/11 began to have a transfigured existence, because it was found in the Bible, and if 9/11 was there, then behold, America was too. Good news? HYes and no. 9/11 had already an uneven track record. Suspicions raised by architects, A&E, combined with an entire underground of surreptitious science, subverted and misreported by the press, underground trains and cities, military bases with unmentionable technologies cast doubt on the official narrative of events. But when the news becomes an archetype something beyond manipulation of facts is at hand.

You may wonder what this is about, but the bare facts include a speech and prayer George Washington made and led on April 30, 1789 convening the first full session of the new constituted government in New York city, the capital at that time. He was inaugurated at Ground Zero, now called Federal Hall Time and place are implicated in that the time was the first duly constituted nation, and place because the location of the prayer service was the same as what is known as St. Paul's chapel at ground zero. What Washington said is relevant, warning that, "smiles of Heaven can never be expected on a nation that disregards the eternal rules of order and right which Heaven itself has ordained," which seems perhaps perfunctory for the time, but by 9/11 becomes as laden with significance as some of the statements of Eisenhower about space invasion and government and business cohabitation.

The nice thing is we can leave Washington there for 212 years, says Tome Dashel, who had the honor of putting America in the Bible that many years later, because the significance of that time and place were more than doubled when the 9/11 attack coincided with both, first because the attack was against the time of that constitution at the place of the chapel. Afterward much celebration was made of the Miracle of the chapel's survival, the only building

left standing around the trade center, not a window broken in the blast of the building's collapse. What save the chapel was a tree between it and the collapse that sheltered it, a sycamore tree, but without becoming botanists a tree suffices. This tree did and did not survive. It is kept as a bronze reconstruct in the roots which hang in the center. That these roots resemble rather the spider of Bilbao would be better left unmentioned. Its stump also is preserved in form. More honor is don to this tree than to many people. ☐ The Trinity Root Today

In September 2005, a two ton bronze sculpture memorializing the surviving root of the fallen **sycamore** tree that shielded St. Paul's Chapel [Completed in 1766, it was known primarily before Sept. 11 as the place where George Washington prayed on April 30, 1789, the day he was inaugurated as president .] from debris on 9/11 was installed in the south courtyard of T…

☐ Installation of the Trinity Root

The root was created to memorialize the surviving root of the fallen **sycamore** tree that shielded St. Paul's Chapel, across the street from Ground Zero, from debris on 9/11.

There is also a statute of Washiongton at the Federal Hall now, four blocks from ground zero, so any visitor can see in embryo the point that Washington was there, but so was the destruction

Outside the walls of information control however, the chapel speaks more of judgment that salvation, since it highlights the destruction of the 7 or so buildings surrounding

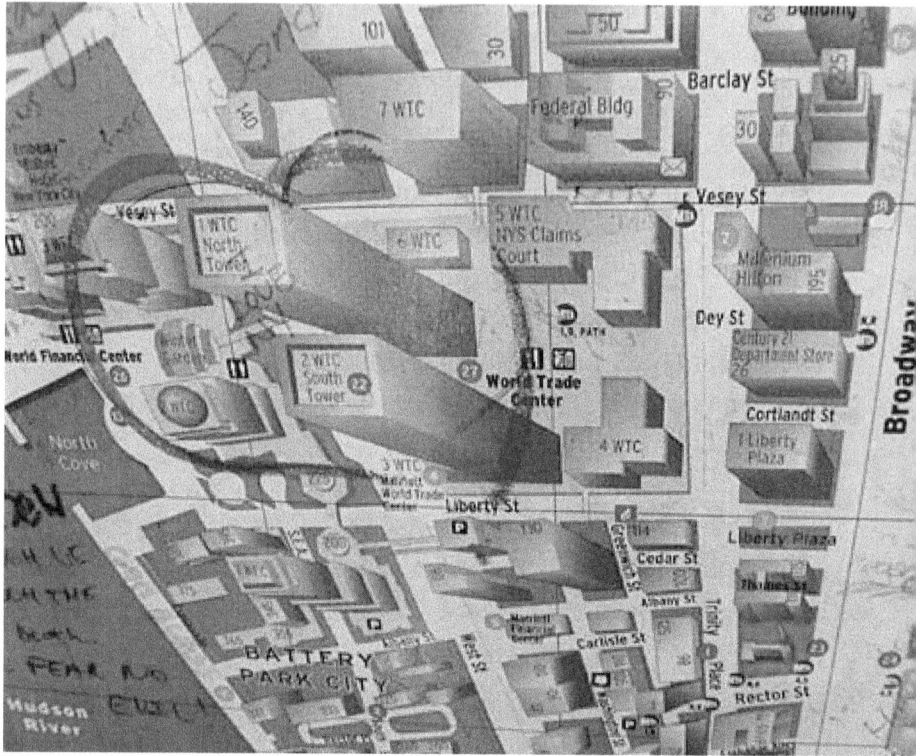

So the sycamore tree is a big deal because it preserved the chapel build in 1766 where Washington went after to pray after his inaugural, where he said: Washington's speech 30 apr 1789

Miracle of the sycamore: "*This stump is all that remains of a 100 - year-old Sycamore that once stood in the northwest corner of St. Paul's churchyard. The tree was toppled on September 11th, 2001, when the collapse of the World Trade Center sent tons of debris hurtling towards the church, including a large steel beam from the*

North Tower. Miraculously, the Chapel's trees shielded from dam and not a single pane of glass was broken through the church."
"In 2005, renowned sculptor Steve Tobin worked with tree experts to preserve the original Sycamore stump that you see here at St. Paul's." (From the Plaque Below the Stump)

It would be as though the wind blew leaves into words on lawns and streets, and the sea washed up shells and painted sand to verb, the fire of forests burned tree words tha spelled these things, the wind blew clouds in sentences, earthquakes split words towering thousands of feet down, word chasms, but still they would not hear.

Notes:

-**James Laughlin** (1914-1997) published many modern writers. "Above the City" first appeared in the yearly anthology of *New Directions 9* next to Henry Miller's essay on Rimbaud, "When Do Angels Cease To Resemble Themselves?" Pound told him here. See this memorial by Kenneth Patchen.
-**Keats and Cortez**: It was really Balboa.
-**Nassim Nicholas Taleb**: "Strangely, my book *Fooled by Randomness*, published a week before September 11, 2001, had a discussion of the possibility of a plane crashing into my office building. So I was naturally asked to show "how I had predicted the event. I didn't predict it-it was a chance occurrence" (*The Black Swan*. New York: Random House, 2007, 153-54).
-**John Gardner**: "Beowulf looks like a fish. "*Conversations with John Gardner*. Edited by Allan Chavkin. Jackson: U of Mississippi Press. 1990, 149.
-**B-25**: Published analysis shows that the reason the B-25 did not bring down the Empire State Building has to do with its

construction and that the weight of impact was 60 to 100 times greater at the WTC. Why this did not trigger an awareness in the builders of the WTC is too much after the fact. It wasn't a mistake as much as a blind spot, an omission, a cost savings, an optimism, so even though the B-25 Bomber sounds big it was small compared to the Boeing 767 airliners, which had full fuel tanks.

Pergamon Altar at the 2008 Denver Convention

What's wrong with George Washington ascending to heaven on the Capitol Dome? Who are the gods behind the gods of the Clinton-Bush-Obamas? There are, 23 zodiacs in D.C. alone. Not only Greek Athena, Poseidos, Hermes, Vulcan, Demeter, but Ishtar's face on cookies and idols of stone from those earlier pantheons were broken. Judeo-Christian scripture makes the breaking of these gods its prime tenet in Abraham. That's behind the story of Nimrod, that early attempt at antichrist, throwing Abraham in the

furnace. Abraham disrespected the gods. What's the connection between the Greco/Roman and Ishtar's Babylon and Washington? We get to find out in a new age of myth.

The spectacle is beautiful and awe inspiring.

A piece or two still missing in the New Washington Order Welcomes Lincoln to Heaven too. This Washington is the one whose deification John Adams and Benjamin Rush protested against. **Myth immigration** is an acquired taste. Shame on E Pluribus for being pagan? The coins of ancient Israel were inscribed "Jerusalem the Holy," but the motto on the dollar bill doesn't say, "Gather Together In One All Things In The Messiah, both in heaven and on earth in Him." It says the capstone to the end of the world waits to be fitted. Washington gropes to a preprogramed seclorum end. But it is not of the Son of Psalm 2, Kiss the Son whose kingdom is set upon the holy hill. This Washington seclorum sounds more like Hosea 13.2, the work of craftsmen where the sacrificers of men kiss the calves. Calf kissing and human sacrifice are used heavily downtown at the Uruk hotel on Kidney St. by the Capitol of the severed head where Ishtar lives, shall we say. Down here in D. C. the Capitol Dome represents mythic control, pieces of a New World Rising from a sea once shunned along with what raises itself to heaven with George Washington in the funnel of the Dome, sucking up to the miscegenate gods. They swirl, they swirl, they swirl, but then comes the sound of their demise.

As Beautiful as spacious skies,
the Inner Babylon,
Azure Isis presides
at the Obama Democratic Convention.

The Islamic caliphate of the ISIS White House began with the appearance of Ishtar in Denver 2008 as a holographic eidolia. This emboldened ISIS immigration to America. At the inaugural of 2008 the Islamic training camps in Mexico and Tennessee were a far fancy as much as the mass migrations taking Europe. But pawns are not the enemy. What's the difference between the supreme religious-political empire of a caliphate and Rome, Babylon, England or America?

When that putative President stood in the Ishtar Gate of the Denver acceptance speech, behind him appeared a mock up of the altar of Zeus of the Pergamon Gates. He clutched his hanuman monkey god in his pocket, a little like the image of Shiva at CERN. It was as if the gods of caliphaty brought Ishtar's promise to the podium: "touch me here, touch me there, and I will give you riches beyond the telling." Dictates of old Babylon handed down governments conceived as merchants in all sorts of blue clothes and embroidery. Ezekiel portrays the ships of Tarshish, their caravans for market (Ez. 27.24-5) as if they were the merchants of souls of Revelation 18. But Ishtar didn't want to possess either Barak or Gilgamesh personally; she wanted their office of President, King. Commerce delivered them into the hand of her love dressed in blue with dyed attire on her heads, clothed most gorgeously with the lustfulness of horses in the bruising of her teats, that "they shall take away thy nose and thine ears (Ez. 23.25). In the language of *Gilgamesh*, she was a lion in the pit, a horse hobbled in mud, a goatherd turned to a wolf, a bird that fell. The man himself would be discarded. But Ishtar brought death. NOW you know why Washington became the sponsor of ISIS. Barak had seen the Altar of Pergamos, a copy of the frieze of Gigantomachy in Berlin along with the Ishtar Gate. His team served this as the promise of abundance in *the azure of pure spirituality.* How many likenesses we need not know. **Ishtar** in a beta test**, said to the tempted gardener,**

> "Now, touch me where you dare not, touch me here
> touch me where you want to, touch me here."

(Gilgamesh, Ferry, 31),

ISIS wants not only wants to visit, it wants to rule! When the American nominee had visited the Pergamos museum on the new Babylonian border, that is, during his trip to and momentous speech in Berlin just before, he saw Pergamos and the Ishtar Gate together and joined them in a combined act of genius in Denver. Baghdad, Babylon, Rome.

Just to bring us up to date on Isis, she's an Egyptian, but Ishtar, the goddess of sex and war is Akkadian, née Babylonian, the PR arm of the Babylon altars and gates stolen and taken to old Germany in the 19th century. They called them archeological sites. Who doubts that if the Germans could also have taken Isis but couldn't catch her? So the modern ISIS Germany's allure, if confused, is still the original queen mother, but Ishtar is a mere strumpet, to split straws. Ishtar's sign was the lapis and the lion, blue and gold. In *Gilgamesh* she was "the door through which the cold gets in." She would turn you to a frog. This explains foreign policy.

How did the Islamic caliphate of ISIS take Ishtar to Denver and then to the Democratic White House to fly its flag? The nominated Obama first visited the Pergamos museum in that capital of the new Babylonian state of Berlin Germany on his trip and momentous speech just before Denver 2008. He brought Pergamos and the Ishtar Gate home in a combined act of genius. Baghdad, Babylon, Rome, Berlin, Denver were the stops**, but not in words.**

Myths and men are easy confused. Germany stole Ishtar, the *public relations* goddess of Babylon, and moved her to Berlin in the 1930s masked as an archaeological site. Who doubts they would have taken Egyptian Isis too, the Queen of Heaven whose altars and gates Jeremiah overthrew, or Astarte, in other words the goddess Ishtar. **One and all, plurbis.** Not to scare you too badly, the Sumerian, Akkadian, Babylonian and Assyrian empires native to modern Iraq had taken these gods from Sumer. Since Isis is the original queen mother but Ishtar a strumpet, modern ISIS in Berlin is Ishtar with a confused allure. Ishtar's sign was the lapis and the lion, blue and gold. The ancient *Gilgamesh* poem calls her foul, "the door through which the cold gets in." She would turn you to a frog, which became shadow Washington policy. ***This* Ishtar as Isis was invited to the Democratic national convention in Denver 2008.** You can see her altar in the blue light podium from which Obama spoke.It's a one stop shop. Gilgamesh 2500 B.C, Babylon 600 B.C, Berlin 1930, Denver 2008. If you think the seven hills of Washington, D. C. replace Rome, and the great white whore that sits on many waters is New York, not Babylon, it must comfort to finally find the United States in the Bible. Rome is there. Babylon is there. *Russia* is there. "This myth has inclined us

to Christianize many pagan aspects of our culture" The Novus Ordo Seclorum list of New Order pagan gods is sprawled all over the Capitol Dome and American currency. Boyd (13). had the good sense not to name this contradiction,

Altar of Pergamos in Berlin

Constructive chaos in the myth of the World Below the Dome
encompasses all these mythic structures of control we cannot see.
These symbols reveal the Novus Ordo Seclorum seal of America in
her sweet Golden Age of Hesiod and Homer had gone to brass.
The harvests of this were Apollo, Apollyon, and Abaddon. From
Nimrod the harvest of ISIS, ISIL came along, extending the
caliphate of the Levant! Myth says the cargo of golden Osiris was
already there inside the Washington Monument. Not only does
ISIS want to visit, she wants to rule.

Way back in old Jerusalem they baked cakes with Ishtar's face
(*Jeremiah* 44), which captives saw after the fall of Jerusalem as they
marched into the inner city of Babylon through the Ishtar
gate. **What is inner Babylon?** Indeed you ask. **Who is Ishtar** that
she should be invited to a surrogate reign in America? The
president's men could not have read what Gilgamesh said when
Ishtar invited *him* into her arms. "Give me your semen; plant your
seed in the body of Ishtar. Abundance will follow riches beyond the
telling" (*Gilgamesh*. David Ferry, 29).

Babylon to Berlin to Denver were her stops, **but not in
words;** images revealed the *Novus Ordo Seclorum* of the American
seal, soul of the sweet Golden Age of Hesiod and Homer gone to
brass. The three harvests of this golden age were Apollo, Apollyon,
and Abaddon. From Nimrod to America came the harvest of ISIS,
ISIL, the caliphate of the Levant! The myth says the golden ego of
Osiris was already there.

There is more than one attempt afoot to break dimensions, counting in antiquity the legends of the stolen Sumerian stone Tablets of Destiny, some acoustic cavitations, and the lapis lazuli box/burial/technology of Gilgamesh's grave in the Euphrates, the Fermi collider outside Chicago supposedly causing the sighting of phantom jets at O'Hare, but also the blind unbuilt original at Waxahachie, Tx, not to speak of the three times life size collider planned by China in the next decade. Don't forget the Ark of Gabriel. These soap operas of science will come true if we wish it. The great science of *this* denouement gives the impression, from the publication of this article, that there is much interest in the statement that the cause of the Iraq War-II was to steal technology from Iraq Museum used to build the Tower of Babel and "take" heaven on a parallel track to CERN.

Dante's vision of Satan boring a wormhole in Earth's crust was labeled *nonfiction* because it doesn't *appear* fictional if CERN is the main character with rituals to unleash. We all have foibles. CERN might be flipped, split in two with a 10.0 earthquake. Bodies infected with geoengineered nano particles or evidence that much of the solar system was devastated in the *katabole* is or is not Solzhenitsyn-like romance before the fact. I settle for the memory of the king of Babylon

> *whose pomp is brought down to the grave.*
> *The noise of viols, the worm spread under him,*
> *the worms covering him.*

And also of the king of Tyre,
> *a fire from within him devours he who is brought to ashes in the sight of all.*

Isaiah 14, Ezekiel 28.

Another note, these worms are like the subterres that slice through rock like a nuclear powered 2000 degree Fahrenheit earthworm. Unfortunately the links are not live in the published version so you can see them in the supplement.

The eight axes in a cross section of CERN intend to break the dimensions separating worlds. The image links to one offered in Alien Sky 55.11 which further study connects the relation of the reconstruction of the golden age of Saturn with CERN as an idea of Anthony Patch (CERN Conspiracy, Canary Cry Radio, Youtube, 10/2/15, 39.15f) that depends first on what is called the Golden Age of the Thunderbolts Project I. That is *before* the planets of our solar system assumed the orbits they now attain. Earth, Mars, Venus and Saturn in this theory were in such a line that Saturn blocked the sun, except for solar crescents that formed on its quadrants. CERN is said to seek to reform the strong electrical bond between the planets that existed then. How the golden age was **Kataboled, or disrupted,** is not a part of the hypothesis, but is touched on below.

It is mighty unbelievable unless you build pathways in your brain to sustain it with various points of recognition. You must be able to sustain the difference between real and fictional (speculative) pathways in this. Patch compares the physics of the Nazi Bell, the North and South poles of Saturn and CERN in the electrical reconnection of earth with the south pole of Saturn using a plasma conduit. A spiral (aureole) at the South pole of Saturn is supposed generated by the supposed *synchrotron* particle accelerator at the North pole, naturally occurring, with a hexagonal shape. Two oppositely moving clouds of energy contained in the hexagon similar to the movement of red mercury in the Nazi bell, spin in opposite directions. The large Hadron Collider, (again) like the massive *synchrotron* accelerator the North pole of Saturn that connects through the gaseous body of Saturn to the south pole. The electric plasma takes the form of a helical shape that looks like DNA. Thus the secret mission of CERN is to connect the helical plasma conduit between the north and south poles of Saturn CERN with the large Hadron collider in order to reconnect Saturn and earth in the same fashion that existed during the golden age. What do you think you can do about that? Throw up your hands and say woe is me? Let me just say it's like the little guy with the doll puppy who comes into the meeting to sell toys, we should say he thinks he's coming in, but listen to what he gets to hear: "you may think you're coming in, but you're not, you're going out." here

Where is your inner Babylon? *Indeed you ask.* Back in old Jerusalem they baked cakes with Ishtar's face (*Jeremiah* 44) to greet the captives as they marched into the inner city through the Ishtar gate after the fall of Jerusalem. **Captivity has a soft side for sweets.** You will be greeted at FEMA camp with treats. Who is Ishtar that she should have a surrogate in America? *There you go again.* The president's men did not read what Gilgamesh said when Ishtar invited *him* into her arms. "Give me your semen; plant your seed in the body of Ishtar. Abundance will follow riches beyond the telling" (*Gilgamesh.* David Ferry, 29).

Gilgamesh is not a freedom saint. He rejects the goddess harlot but takes every betrothed bride before her wedding. In the allegory he is Washington too. This means Panama, Vietnam, Algeria, all nations in person or proxy taken. All wives and daughters subverted. The difference is that **Gilgamesh knows supernatural coitus with the goddess steals his manhood**. Washington thinks it's exempt.

These temptations sheared right through the Denver stage and blew up in another dimension. Nominee Obama spoke from the middle of the gate (in the image) the German archeologists had taken to Berlin. This was his Acceptance of a lot more than the Democratic nomination. "Abundance will follow, riches without telling," unless the procession of lapis and aurochs and cedar before the wall of lions is telling. Unless he didn't pull away like that sport Daniel did from Nebuchadnezzar's gods, or Abraham who broke Nimrod's. Then the lions on the Gate, symbols of Ishtar, had their mouths shut.

Are you glad you were here to see it at least, the movies of tyranny in the guise of a lizard with a four chambered heart, six fingers, toes and a spine, and a space alien from the stars as its General? That's even bigger than Washington, the el archon. All the flushable gods of the Capitol Dome who swell their minds in the global play turn human hopes to fantasy. Clown Earth politics and religion serve up the rare *Novus Ordo* of myth from the bowel of this heaven. Except it is a toilet bowl. According to this wisdom toilet government officials have no personal identity, evil is banal, and the turds are there to make the human superfluous, to hold office till Osiris comes. But drain the swamp, the feet of man standing on earth is Messiah's province in Psalm 8, and man's. It still is. Ordained.

Elite discoveries of pre-Adamite tech machines from ancient Sumerian sites stored in Mosul with the Lapis Gilgamesh have no more empirical evidence than the Ark of Gabriel or Scalia's Ash. If it is so that the Ark of Gabriel went Feb 2016 to the old Builder Palace of the Puradu Fallen that must have left a lot of 12 ft tall dehydrated pot-bellied long heads ajar. Where they came from is in your Bible and below, but all the buildings flash froze about the same time as the electrical scouring of Mars. Technologies however were preserved.

Obama, Clapper and Kerry fleeing the Russian hack came to these labs under ice in 2016 and confirmed every genetic and financial mutation. Flood-reduced Puradu from the eminent ancient sources at Qumran mentioned that same mutation. Elite authority Edgar Cayce said it was Atlantis. Graham Hancock gave the Platonic date of 9,600 B.C. Enoch said, "they sinned against birds, and beasts, and reptiles, and fish" (*Enoch* 6-7), "corrupted alike men and cattle and beasts and birds and everything that walked the earth" (*Jub.* 5.1-2). That makes the mutating grosbeaks of the D.C. Beltway a little tame, but fake news builds the tale. *After* the American underground linked sex crimes with "discoveries" of Antarctic Atlantis, not just physics and astronomy but anthropology, pyramids, shelf-splits, underground lakes, earth changes, ice melts, cracks, glaciers broke off. DARPA's underground *Neuschwabenland* (c. 1938), Admiral Byrd's disastrous HighJump (1947), 19th century hollow earth paradigms turned solid, post 1947. America of course is a way of saying Europe. Elites manage the whole world to succumb to its control. It's nice to think of Ishtar as a whore if you love orgy. The gardener knew not to "eat the rotten food / having been taught to eat the wholesome," so she turned the gardener into a frog. This meant symbolically for Gilgamesh that either you have your spirit broken and your mind imprisoned, or, as happens when *he too* rejects her, be confronted with the bull of heaven loosed by her rage. These supernatural force gods were thought to be mere fairy tales in 2008, before they were unleashed today. Ishtar's complaint against Gilgamesh, King of Uruk (Baghdad) was that "he has found out my foulness" (32). He said,

You are the fire that goes out. You are the pitch
that sticks to the hands of the one who carries the bucket.
You are the house that falls down. You are the shoe
that pinches the foot of the wearer. The ill-made wall
that buckles when time has gone by. The leaky
waterskin soaking the waterskin carrier.

The Obama team may not have known this, or maybe they believed
the promise of abundance. But Ishtar didn't want either Gilgamesh
or Barak personally; she only wanted the office of the president. In
the language of the poem, a lion in the pit, the horse hobbled in mud,
the goatherd turned to a wolf, the bird that fell, the man himself
would be discarded. How many likenesses we need not know, **but
when Ishtar said to the tempted gardener,**

"Now, touch me where you dare not, touch me
here, touch me where you want to, touch me here."
(*Gilgamesh*, Ferry, 31)

he knew not to "eat the rotten food / having been taught to eat the
wholesome." I hope **Nobody** thinks from this that Ishtar is a whore.
It's not nice to call names. Once rejected she turned the gardener into
a frog. You thought I was going to say king. It was only because she
was hungry. The choice symbolically for Gilgamesh was, have your
spirit broken and your mind imprisoned, or, as happens when *he
too* rejects her, be confronted with the bull of heaven loosed by her
rage. Ishtar's complaint against Gilgamesh, King of Uruk
(Baghdad) was that "he has found out my foulness" (32).

You are the fire that goes out. You are the pitch
that sticks to the hands of the one who carries the bucket.
You are the house that falls down. You are the shoe

that pinches the foot of the wearer. The ill-made wall
that buckles when time has gone by. The leaky
waterskin soaking the waterskin carrier.

Gilgamesh's rejection of harlotry is opposed by his free rein in taking every other form of woman, which in the allegory means country, Panama, Vietnam... from brides before their marriage, to all wives and daughters, but Gilgamesh recognizes that **supernatural coitus steals manhood**. Why do we always talk in code? Bull? These forces anyway shared the Denver stage **through the gate** German archeologists took to Berlin. The president spoke from the middle of the image in his acceptance. "Abundance will follow, riches without telling," all of course, with the procession of lapis and aurochs and cedar before the walls of lions.

It was a one stop shop. Gilgamesh, 2500 B.C, Babylon 600 B.C, Berlin, 1930, Denver, 2008. At least the President was not a spoil sport like Daniel who did to Nebuchadnezzar's gods what Abraham did to Nimrod's, where the lions on the Gate, symbols of Ishtar, had their mouths shut.

*Critics resist supernaturalism until science posits a **divergent hybrid species** whose headboarded elongated skulls are found in the thousands. Headboarding is also psychological. The words transhuman science echo transhuman sacrifice, implying that the breaking of transhuman idols would be as appalling to them as Abraham's disrespect of idols was to Nimrod. Science has as its end the breaking of man, making him as his own god-idol worshiping himself,that being his immortality. Nimrod, a shadowy figure linked to Gilgamesh as ruler of the city of Uruk, opponent of God, a Hunter in the Face of God, unbelievably had his remains* *dug up by the American quartermaster corp in the Iraq war to be cloned. Perhaps it is better to say Nimrod/Gilgamesh's remains were stolen from the French-German archeologists because of some heretofore unsuspected weaponry.*

-- <u>Tomb of Gilgamesh found,</u> **reportedly** <u>sequestered</u>

--<u>Middle East giants</u>

--<u>DMT</u>, **a** <u>nootropic</u> **smart drug cognitive enhancers with monotomic gold**

Smithsonian cover up of giants

How would classicists and Form theorists handle the redaction

of supernaturalist government Elohists who seek to revive, literally resurrect and scroll from the graves impossible supernatural weapons?

2.

The United States is not even symbolically mentioned in the Bible. Rome is there. Babylon is there. *Russia* is there.

"This [American Christian nation] myth has inclined us to Christianize many pagan aspects of our culture" says Boyd (13). A Novus Ordo Seclorum - New Order for the Ages - with pagan gods sprawled all over the Capitol Dome and currency- is an awkward contradiction for a Christian nation. Boyd had the good sense not to name the pagans of constructive chaos behind the myth of the dome. **The World Below the Dome** is symbolic of all these mythic structures we cannot see. So we may take our dome as a godsend of revelation even if it is really holding us in a hiding in the holes and rocks of caves.

Shame that *E Pluribus Unum* is pagan? The motto on the dollar bill doesn't say, "Gather Together In One All Things In The Messiah, both in heaven and on earth in Him." The coins of ancient Israel were inscribed "Jerusalem the Holy," but Americans grope to a *seclorum* end, not of the Son of Psalm 2, *Kiss the Son whose kingdom is set upon the holy hill. The seclorum* sounds more like Hosea 13.2, *the work of craftsmen where the sacrificers of men kiss the calves.* Calf kissing and human sacrifice is being pursued downtown at the Uruk hotel of the Kidney, or the Capitol of **The Severed Head** and **Ishtar**, we shall say.

Why disrespect the American gods when no body believes in them? Do you follow Zeus? Myth is such an acquired taste. What's wrong with George Washington ascending to heaven on the Capitol Dome inhabited by the gods Athena, Poseidon, Hermes, Vulcan, Demeter? Well, only that Judeo-Christian scripture makes the *breaking* of these gods its prime tenet. Not just the Greek gods either, but Ishtar's face broken on those cookies and idols of stone whose earlier versions of Greek pantheon were all broken by Abraham. That's why Nimrod threw him in the furnace, disrespect of the gods. What's the connection between the Greek/Roman gods and Ishtar's Babylon in America? We find out in a new age of myth.

Abraham's Hammer

Down in D. C. the dome represents mythic control. If pieces of the Capitol are one day sold as the Berlin Wall was (for the movies are taking out the White House and Capitol most summers), *come and buy, come and buy* -- vendors will have the same world they've always had, that is, *whoever is unjust, let him be unjust still* (Johnny Cash). Pieces of new world rising, shunned along with what raises itself to heaven with George in the funnel of the Capitol Dome, sucking up to the miscegenate gods, will swirl. They swirl, they swirl and *then* comes the sound. I'm saying that there has been a takeover and all the pieces of *this* new world shunned by Abraham are the New Washington Order that Welcomes Lincoln to Heaven, but it is not the one we know, or John Adams and Benjamin Rush, who protested against Washington's deification. What could we have against our Fathers, or against what they did or didn't do? Back masked, *E Pluribus Unum* becomes the cord its adversaries use to strangle them.

The other important mixture of science and myth involves the Iraq War II where the alleged covert purpose was to steal the technology from the Iraq Museum that Nimrod and/or Gilgamesh used in building the Tower of Babel, which was not a building exactly, more of an antenna that broadcast the EM frequencies we call scalar and were an attempt to "take" the heaven, whatever that could mean. Of course what it means is destroy the heaven, break the dimensions. The attempt failed because of outside interference, so called, which is one way of saying that the technology was good. What exactly it was of course was the purpose of its theft by the U.S. c. April 8, 2003. The best guess is that it represents a parallel track to the supercollider at CERN to break time, break the dimensions, find dark matter, let loose the hordes, in other words. When technology sounds like myth and myth like technology the simplistic principles of empirical science are out of date. All kinds of alternatives to Renown technology exist, especially Disclosure, assigning these discoveries to infiltrators from Sirius, Cassiopeia, Andromeda. And none of these explain parallel phenomena such as the buried super cites on the sea floor off of Japan at Yonaguni Jima, sunk in toto, more engineering projects of the builders of Babel. Those busy builders!

I began to revisit the reopening of the multidimensional gates located everywhere from Sedona to Bolivia when I became aware that that is exactly what CERN seeks to do in this present run, to force open whatever tissue of glue, gravity, veil stands between what they believe is this dimension and the other, serial dimensions of dark matter they think they are measuring, but can't see. The overt religious fervor of this in the statue at the facility, the odd reports of paranormal effects reported around it, the opera Dance of Destruction, filmed to celebrate this run, with its creepy effects, break dancing taken from My Pet Goat II and the applause on all the CERN videos whenever they complete a run, like a moonshot, factor taking the subject as the Days of Noah as an explanation, you know, when people were eating and drinking and giving in marriage right up until the rains came. Shiva the destroyer is a pun on the rains, in this case the doors opening, the gates thinning, to result in, and now here the effects might be a wee speculate, the coming of giants to eat you, the rising from the bed of the Euphrates of the horsemen of Revelation and the seven seals. This last quickly exhausts the viewer.

Back then to reality, or what we call alternative reality, comes the purpose for the Iraq War, which, all other causes notwithstanding, was to retrieve from the Museum of Iraq artifacts Saddam had dug up, and which the American special forces retrieved on the first day of the war, these constituting DNA formulas of Nimrod, to study how he, "began to become," a necessity for transhumans who wish the same upon themselves and must be considered another arm of the destroying Shiva at CERN. This explains why the Americans allowed the looting of the museum after, to cover their tracks. But Shiva has five or six arms. The other booty, flown out by helicopter by night, selected by the American ambassador who was on site to see to it, was, and you will appreciate how this is the counterpart to CERN, the control mechanism and power source of the Tower of Babel, viz. the technology of the fallen angels. That there is a theology anthropology behind all this you can ferret out yourself in the sources of Tom Horn and Steve Quayle and their associates. This bit about the Curator of the Iraq Museum comes 47.15-55.39f in their On the Path of the Immortals "

Allied to this in some odd way, the interview of Alex Jones with Louis Lefebvre about Pet Goat II argues that this is throwing the illuminati imagery back in the face of the elites to cause consciousness, but consider whether it doesn't do the opposite, merely to confirm those images by using them. Any pub is good pub. These are very like those images of Tomorrow Land in Rio and that to come in Atlanta, which pose as initiatory rites to invoke multidimensionals through the portal, so also allied to CERN, presumably to be announced on CNN. The coming cannibalism of the giants to be let loose, "the land devours its inhabitants"

(*Numbers*) should be viewed as even more mental and spiritual than it will be physical devouring. If you wonder at all these precursors to the events to come, what they call predictive programming, it is arguably a technique of propaganda to preprogram a reserve data drop before the effect, so that it mimics precognition, or foretelling, and is recognized and therefore more readily triggers belief in that section of the brain where these lodge.

So Bush-Obama Amer-uca, land of the feathered serpent, learns to jump space through orbs with ancient portal technology stolen from Saddam at the same time as CERN does, but with suspicion that there are colliders in the US anyway. You just have to look underground. Good luck with that, as much as even getting onto the Bradshaw Ranch, the Sedona Portal, since it is now owned by the Gov.

When Gilgamesh crept into my work on ThoughtGottens and Oracle Binding, and the first awareness of the Lapis box that was said to be recovered from his remains, there is no list or the number of these portals yet, but Mount Graham and the Four Corners in addition to Sedona are being bought up. Of course Dulce on the Archuleta is already in the portfolio. Today you can hear about Donald Trump, civil and financial unrest and immigration and receive that there is a higher and lower sort, that immigration coming in to those ports. Well that's what it means to be eating and drinking right up until the flood comes. Another arm of this Shiva opening portals would be the Vatican offering homes to the space brothers they conjure from de Chardin on to their portal on Mt. Graham, which was brought to us by Senator John McCain. Another portal, but also one masked, or one to mask the work at CERN and at the D. C. government labs with Babel. I almost said Beelzebub. Check the astrobiology here at Baptized Martians, which of course is a joke since, if they have not fallen into sin, as the Vatican suspects, they will baptize us. Then they will kill us. CERN is the consequence of the Vril Society under its occult names. Further research, try dinosaurs at Sedona, suicides at CERN. Fallen seraphim reptilian giants need to be fed. The best news received in the interim is that we are all in a medieval, Roman system of two classes of rulers and peasants. It is so comforting to be a restored peasant after suffering the illusion so long that I was better, something else. My aunt insisted always from an early age that we are all peasants. I have come home to it, knowing that I know nothing of the world and its stratagems, time and its breaking, even if I sue the words, and that I am so unimportant that I can be left alone to live my illusions without interference. It was my own fault for ever thinking otherwise, but we also recognize that is the programming put upon us at birth, in schools, in society, that we matter and that we can do anything. All illusion, all chimera.

Two reigning possibilities, ET vs the Anshei Nephites, have many permutations, but the best one is the simplest, that they are the same, not that the numbers of intelligent parties who have had experience of ET would accept this. Steve Greer had early experience of contact. It became his *raison d'être*, his reason for being, leant significance to his life, although he is a member of the ruling class and not a peasant, which should give pause. Two classes of ET emerge, the android manufacture, programmed life form, chipped and cloned (extended to most Hollywood stars) and the "real" kind that say they are from Andromeda or Sirius and come with benign intent, little Speilbergs, for whom we must enter an age of peace, not war, so earth can have more generations, another neat bifurcation between the real and the unreal to draw participants toward the middle. Even though the Hegelian is decried by all these groups they all use it. The Disclosure effort by all accounts is to come public in an alien war, etc. a false flag event run by the rulers to consolidate ever more power.

Before this all gets lost in the details, none of these are fact, that being that every one of these appearances is black budget, black shelved, sequestered technologies that have been known for years to be thousands of years ahead of what is used on the earth, credited by the Men of Renown, who can take many shapes, littley greys for the Nazis, etc. It is pertinent that Revelation says that this was the beast that was, that is not, then that is and then that is no more, and that this somehow explains the timeline that repeats the days of Noah, for there is plenty of history of these briquettes in ancient times entering human affairs, making fit extensions of themselves, i.e. hybrids, giants. In this there seem three classes, the first angels who fell, their breeding of their race of Anshei Nephites further breeding into giants.

Diffused and disguised effects are to be argued from all of this, that is, radiations, skips and jumps in different directions affecting crime, war, earthquakes, politics, social movements (refugees, chemical plant explosions, Santiago, Chile, bogus nuclear treaties, Hajj stampede, threats of N and S Korea, China, Russia, the all purpose Obama dignitaries and the Pope). It was part of this world illusion that its best and brightest had all done unspeakable things and made bargains to display their beauty and power that made them so shine, but which in actual fact had debased them so far beneath the idea even of a human that they retained only the vestige.

Cited. *The Divine Comedy of Dante Alighieri. Inferno.* Allen Mandelbaum. 1980

Oracle Weimar

Stephen Spender gets out his *Poems* of 1933. Electrosmog lights up the smoke, out of order, out of time. Like a poem moved by dilemmas for its own sake, but no easy kinship for the desolate sweep, it is inscribed as an oracle "For Horst Keller as, a souvenir of Oxford London Berlin from Stephen Spender / **March 11, 1933**."

Spender writes in his Journal *"I* met [Horst] on the Hook of Holland boat once, shortly before Hitler's rise to power,*"* twelve days after the Reichstag fire (27 Feb 1933).

Fast forward to the Colorado late at night, edge of a lunar eclipse, Halloween with fires, rooftops aflame amid calls on civilization to surrender to what it does not believe, that bizarre Earth burrowers, mole prophets claim.

Who can understand an illiterate analogy of seventy five postwar German years to manufacture American peace? Time, upset by its recurrence, brings Weimar out of the smoke with the same "unhappy, pained, gentle creatures who represent the heart of another Germany, and do not understand what is happening to them… peculiar whiteness and stillness of their eyes which seem to have been drained of pigment…How closely I press upon a secret! Why am I always attracted by these desolate spirits?" (Stephen Spender, *Journals, 1939-1983, 30).*

esWhich do you prefer, 20th century prewar Germany or 21st century prewar America? Stephen says, *Watch the hawk with an indifferent eye,* that almost *won War on the sun* until the *hands, wings, are found (Poems, 1933, 11).* As if it were the best of all possible worlds with the Trojan Horse outside the gate, Leviathan come to land, we find the eyes and hands, and then the tongue.

Hitler's "rise" ended in March 1933 after the Reichstag adopted the Enabling Act of 1933. President Paul von Hindenburg appointed Hitler Chancellor on 30 January 1933 after elections and intrigues. Then Hitler used The Enabling Act to **constitutionally exercise dictatorial power** without legal objection.

Which do you prefer, 20th century prewar Germany or 21st century prewar America? Stephen says, Watch the hawk with an indifferent eye, that almost won War on the sun until the hands, wings, are found (Poems, 1933, 11).

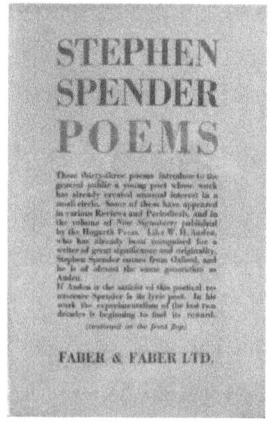

Spender says, "Horst was the son of a general. And now at least four names crowd on to me I remember. Many are aristocrats and often close to the higher ranks of the army. This boy called Horst had a round face with very well-formed features, delicate lips, light blue eye, and brown hair of an almost feathery lightness. He was very quiet and polite and he had some small, out-of-the-way interest – playing the flute or making musical instruments or something.

There's really nothing much more to it than that. He had a scholarship at Oxford and I used to call on him there; we went for walks and I introduced him to Isaiah Berlin. But he never in the least became part of the life at Oxford...**one of those unhappy, pained, gentle creatures who represent the heart of another Germany, and do not understand what is happening to them.** I have touched a deeper chord than I knew here, for Have I not met two or three? Didn't I know very well the peculiar whiteness and stillness of their eyes which seem to have been drained of pigment? These poor ghosts are really beautiful in a sexless way, because, if one is a young man of another country, an exile in one's own, one cannot expect to be virile. How closely I press upon a secret! Way am I always attracted by these desolate spirits?" (*Journal*. 1985, 30)

Keller is dismissed. "Always just as gentle, just as isolated [with] a restlessness that never ceased." But **the poor ghosts, Stephen later says, stand as oracles for Americans** of "peculiar whiteness, drained of pigment." "Most of these poets and writers...delivered their sad advice on the literary life which I was now just about to enter, like ghosts in purgatory, conscious of the relative failure of their illusions" (*World On Worlds*, 89).

For Horst Keller
as a souvenir of Oxford
London & Berlin from
Stephen Spender.
March 11th, 1933

As if appointing a board of directors Auden had assigned Spender to be the poet at Oxford, and Isherwood got to be the novelist, grasping at illusion not compulsion. Escape from the Weimar illusion fell to Dylan Thomas, drunk all the time, and Faulkner too, or Edith Sitwell immersed in some depth psychology of esoteric Jung. The lords of lit dismiss its victims as Americans dismiss the present,

Spender says, with "the sustained gentle sense of unhappiness"
(31). So much signifying of Horst Keller naked, dismissed for lack
of philosophic depth as all poets and critics scourge each other.
Pound called Yeats *The Tower* putrid. Hemingway called Spender
squeamish, and why not? It is the counterpart of the bullying
Stephen received, "My parents kept me from children who were
rough...their knees tight on my arms. / I feared the salt coarse
pointing of those boys" *(Poems XII)*.

**Cloistered Stephen and Keller prophesy how we live in
Weimar before the fall,** "coracles with faces painted on"
(Spender, Poems, III). Even if the Reich-stag burns in the Twin
Towers morphed to a propaganda tool, these are just mirages of the
digital, like a new species of digitalis that poisoned Van Gogh's
brain which he was given for seizures. His brain saw a color shift
which produced the yellow period, haloes around
lights. Xanthopsia fools like propaganda. Our seizures, after
creation of the group mind, when the news is offered by Yahoo
headlines, have no word for who will destroy the world. Oracle
ambiguous. Electronic designs "more beautiful and soft than any
moth / With burring furred antennae feeling its huge path" *(Poems,
XXVII)*. This is Weimar's *Childhood's End*, catalyzed by the
beast that comes from its ship in 50 years! So it's not just England
naked and the world where "all things are naked and opened unto
the eyes" as the saint in Stephen would say. He could have written
a *Psalm*, "I am poured out like water and all my bones are out of
joint...I may count all my bones.*" (Psalm 22.14)*. England is
America without water to cross. England echoes America and
America China, India, Ukraine, Egypt, Japan.

The Globe is the world, the splendid coracle says, absolutely guarded in its superiority of being, "three stand naked: the new,

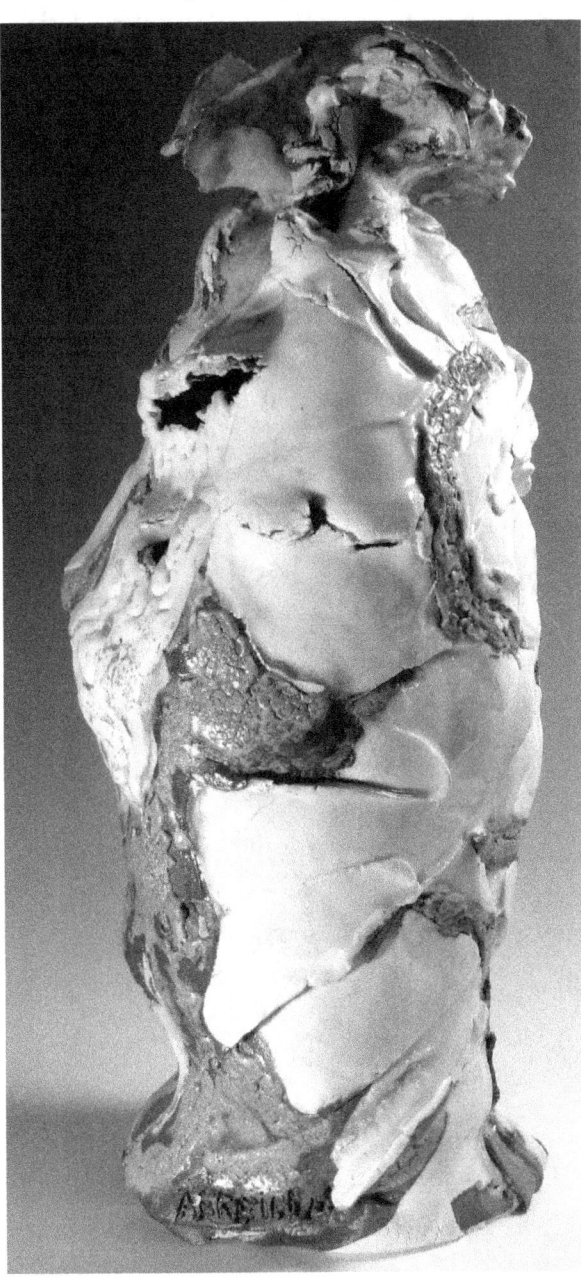

bronzed German, / the communist clerk, and myself, being English" (*Poems*, XIV in 1929). All for one and one for all. HBO. "I'm haunted by these images, / I'm haunted by their emptiness" *(Poems,* XVI). Who in Wii America lives in the shadow of war? None! Just like Weimar. QED! The quiescence of disassociation of what is right before the eyes was all along prepared by predictive programming, whether falling towers or chimera super heroes, men of renown, so the eye could say it had seen it all before. Spender, a decade before, sees "The prisoners / Turned massive with their vaults and dark with dark" (*Poems*, XX).

The oracle "throws up strange shapes, broad curves / And parallels clean like the steel of guns" (*Poems*, XXVI). Everybody feels empowered by the need not to remember. Maps, addresses, time are no more. Weimar does not believe the porcelain words of "Slanting iron hair pattern no stigmata" (*Poems*, XXXI), "that program of the antique Satan / Bristling with guns on the indented page" (*Poems*, XXXIII). The machine of war in three worlds: apocalypse heaven, earth and hell. Choose at least one. That's what you get when their knees are tight on your arms and they hold you down, while Chomsky thinks its Hitler from the right with the forces marching, *left, right, left, right*. It's not Hitler coming, or Weimar just back from the Danube, Marlene Dietrich singing, hyperinflation, Balkanization. It's four angels loosed from the Euphrates.

Cited:

Poems. Stephen Spender (Faber and Faber, 1933).

-Xanthopsia. A deficiency of the optical media of the eye, predominating yellow.

-"Putrid." *The Paris Review* interview with Stephen Spender, Winter/Spring 1980.

-Chomsky, see http://louisproyect.org/2010/04/20/weimar-germany-and-contemporary-america-any-parallels/

Opiomes the Domes

WHAT WERE THE ANCESTRAL VOICES prophesying war that
Coleridge heard in a dream?

> *Oh that deep romantic chasm*
> *Ancestral voices prophesying war!*
> *The shadow of the dome of pleasure,*
> *I would build that dome in air,*
> *That sunny dome! Those caves of ice!*
> *And all who heard should see them there,*
> *And all should cry, Beware! Beware!*

They were the starchitectures of Gigantotomy, a lot to take in one,
let alone many: the Tower of Babel, Ishtar Gate, Capitol Dome,
Washington Monument, Nebuchadnezzar's gold statue,

Guggenheim Museum Bilbao, EU Parliament, Denver Airport, the eyes of Oculus Horus in the subway beneath the 9/11 site, a vortex swallowing the globe. Name your own. Goat statues don't count. Shrines more or less equivalent to embodied ideas, political-religious metaphysicals repeat and mimic that sunny dome. But whether the milk of paradise of Coleridge's "Kubla Khan" or the artificial paradises of the French (*Les Paradis artificiels*), "the dreams of a maniac who would replace solid furniture and a real garden by decorative canvas backdrops," it strikes us that Baudelaire, the poet of sulphur flowers, moralizes against artifice as much as William Burroughs is against drugs (*Naked Lunch*). Both reputations go against this grain, but they learned hard, as did Rimbaud who embraced Christ on his death bed.

Starchitectures come to every species. The bizarre Spider of Bilbao and the Blue Horse of Denver live in the shade where Frabel designed glass botanicals, "flowers like the lily, Dogwood, Cherokee Rose and various Orchids recreated in borosilicate glass" (*Life in the Gardens*). Star doctrine says "there is not one single invention of Nature, however subtle or impressive it may be that the human spirit cannot create; no forest of Fontainebleu or moonlit scene that cannot be produced on a floodlit stage; no waterfall that hydraulics cannot imitate so perfectly as to be indistinguishable from the original; no rock that paper-mache cannot copy; no flower that specious taffetas and delicately painted papers cannot rival!"

They do not call themselves Earthitects who turn flowers into glass, trees into gold and fulfill a dozen fantasies from material riches to immortality. Starchitecture is as old as we make it, or find it, the hedge of yellow metal of Claudian, the ambiguity of gold refined from earth, an image of wisdom as deadly as Midas killing the plant with a touch. This vision of reality, a forgery, counterfeit, artifice is what Baudelaire says substitutes the vision for reality itself. The fruit of gold, the glass orchid, immortality satisfy no hunger for food any more than hunger for beauty or life. The fraudulent towers, sculptures and buildings, if we judge by the gold plant, lose all their nature in seeking to touch the sky, to enshrine the starchitects as absurdly as the golden age.

"The dreams of a maniac who would replace solid furniture and a real garden by decorative canvas backdrops," Among many notable leaping frogs of starchitecture the Guggenheim Museum of Bilbao is another airport where these ideas fly in. You might imagine a schedule of arrivals and departures, but more than flights of fancy if we say forces want to take the Horse into Troy.

Guggenheim-Bilbao and EU Parliament-Babel combine with a spider and a siren and the *Blue Horse* of Denver as examples of these visions of reality. Structures read like illustrations, semaphores on the runways of the new age. Anubis and the Denver Murals are signaling. Architects, dubbed "archistars" for their designs, make starchitecture to memorialize themselves, but the coinage suits admirably the works of thousands of years, including the *Trojan Horse* and the *Ishtar Gate*. The Blue Horse in Denver doesn't quite seem demonic enough. Such honor should be reserved for that part human / part beast seen by the Aztecs as the Spanish on horseback. Likewise we interpret today the depictions in ancient Sumer, horses with heads of a lion, hair of a woman, and stingers in their tails as from Bergman's *Seventh Seal* as recombinant mutants of all kinds from USDA labs. The movies long ago replaced the news as sources of current events. Movies and of course the classics. Visiting Anubis, the Jackal-headed death dog that floated down the Thames from Egypt on its world tour, these join the line of iconic figures that dwarf or magnify the past in the guise of bringing art to the masses.

Bring Art to the Masses

In order to better manipulate these structures, committees of starchitects are planning to revive Milton's *Paradise Lost*, Book II, as illustrated by Gustave Dore, that is, *Satan on the Burning Lake*. This is prophetic also of Milton's iconotecture in raising up *Pandemonium* from a bubble pipe, also being prepared by governments for execution.

Michelangelo's "Drunkenness of Noah" is sure to be made an inebriant hologram broadcast to numb the culling of the herd.

Turner's "Angel Standing in the Sun" is on the drawing board for the new millennium in France.

The Denver Airport only needs some further Dante to traverse its underground and show it to be a ship ready for blast off. Denver Airport Elites Escape Earth! Are you ready for blast off? Read this before you go.

News photographers on the Inferno beat, I mean the Dante/Virgil Report, will expose those "two travelers who find the shaggy and gigantic Lucifer at the absolute center of the Earth, embedded up to his waist in ice. The only way they can continue their journey is by climbing down his sides—there is plenty of hair to hold on by— and squeezing through the hole in the ice and so coming to his feet" they climb down the page, "though it is down to his waist, it is up to his feet" (*Inferno* xxxiv, 70f: C. S. Lewis, *The Discarded Image*, 141-2). That hair is needed because directions are reversed and its been cold. Anybody planning to leave should make ready their passport metaphors, hair and all. Whether dome, spaceship, donkey or mule carry their sins aloft or beneath, the epic world is closer than we know. Scale an inch to the miles below.

EDITOR'S NOTES W/LINKS:

Samuel Taylor Coleridge's Kubla Khan: Supposedly Coleridge dreamed up this poem under the influence of opium.
http://en.wikipedia.org/wiki/Kubla_Khan

Starchitecture:

Weird or unconventional structures designed by celebrity architects such as Frank Gehry.
http://en.wiktionary.org/wiki/starchitecture#English

Gigantotomy: figures carved into hillsides such as Mt Rushmore or the Cerne Abbas Giant
http://www.encyclo.co.uk/define/Gigantotomy

Denver Airport: because of its unconventional design the airport has been the subject of a great many conspiracy theories such as "it is the HQ of the New World Order"

http://rationalwiki.org/wiki/Denver_Airport_conspiracy_theory

Blue Mustang: this sculpture of a horse is associated with the theories concerning the Denver Airport. The sculptor himself was killed when the horse fell over on him in his studio.
http://en.wikipedia.org/wiki/Blue_Mustang

European Union Parliament Building a structure often likened to the fable Tower of Babel http://vigilantcitizen.com/sinister-sites-the-eu-parliament/

Tower of Babel: http://en.wikipedia.org/wiki/Tower_of_Babel

Nebuchadnezzar's Gold Statue
http://en.wikipedia.org/wiki/Daniel_2

Ishtar Gate http://en.wikipedia.org/wiki/Ishtar_Gate

Oculus Horus: a public arts project in which strange occult symbols were painted in the subway beneath the World Trade Center http://www.jesus-is-avior.com/Evils%20in%20Government/911%20Cover-up/911_memorial.htm

William S. Burroughs' *Naked Lunch:*
http://en.wikipedia.org/wiki/Naked_Lunch

Hans Godo Frabel: a noted glass artist
http://en.wikipedia.org/wiki/Hans_Godo_Frabel

Ingmar Bergman's *The Seventh Seal*:
http://en.wikipedia.org/wiki/The_Seventh_Seal and can be obtained here: http://www.criterion.com/films/173-the-seventh-seal?q=autocomplete

Michaelangelo's "Drunkeness of Noah": http://art-now-and-then.blogspot.com/2012/09/the-greatest-painting.html

JW Turner's "Angel Standing in the Sun": http://www.tate.org.uk/art/artworks/turner-the-angel-standing-in-the-sun-n00550

Charles Baudelaire's *Les Paradis Artificiels:*
http://en.wikipedia.org/wiki/Les_Paradis_artificiels

Milton's *Paradise Lost* & Pandemonium:
http://en.wikipedia.org/wiki/Paradise_Lost

Hybrid Beastiary.

*Woe to you puppets who say they are leaders of untold other flies
as it were, decamped on the rocks of Isaiah to land. Official
figureheads drew Isaiah tight about America's neck, a rhetorical
noose, as though "Yahweh sent a word to Jacob (Isaiah 9.8), and it
lighted upon America." But the real cause of the apocalypse was
the same as it was for Noah, the systemic corruption of the living
genome. Didn't you know that's what the Flood was about? Oh
dear. Don't you know that right now in every first world
underground lab and military these same creatures are being
made? Does that imply some intelligence spanning thousands of
years sticking its neck out again to have its day? The Day of the
LORD begins in darkness, the evening before what we call the day,
but then comes the light.*

ONCE THERE WAS a genetical singing mouse whose future of
"true godlike intelligence" (Artilect War 180, 183) was not yet out.
Along with tiny voice Mouse came bat wing mouse and human ear
Vacanti mouse (#2). Not to immortalize or sing this mouse was the
moral tragedy of not building gods, for those ephemeral little
lives so worthless, so insignificant," when compared (Artilect War,
186). From this human existence got the drift, "so petty, so trivial,

so banal, so insignificant" (87).

We know all this from reading Hugo, I want to call him Roland de Garis, who blew his horn and said, "from the galactic point of view, would it matter much if the human were wiped out? I think the universe would not give a damn" (89). Why does the physicist quantum quark not reconcile with Fibonacci on these shell and leaf spirals? Order and chaos, yes and no, but wiping out the mouse would be a tragedy. Beam me up Scotty! Save the mouse! Wipe out the man? Why doesn't the transhuman universe give a damn if Kafka does? "Being Cosmist and more intelligent... I suspect that those people [Galactics, have] higher IQs" (Artilect, 89).

More Mouse Wipe Out

We care about this mouse because little man (H) is defunct too: "too stupid, and have too small a brain to speculate on anything, unless it's about their immediate survival" (Artilect 179). Ditto the dumb-bunny baby, ble, ble, ble, the ideal rabbit, Dudeney's cows, honeybees, the "apelike thoughts of chimps." Ditto, but, but if artilect slips, as mouse has accidents and men, and doesn't "develop life-preserving strategies" to avoid falling into a star, then oops "the laws of physics" it removes (Artilect 180). Thus the Absolut of science invents one law and another.
Sensory experiments enhanced a man's nose who could now chat with a devil and smell like a dog.

As mice are men, de Garis and Kurzweil will not need their brains, like Yeats his nymphs and satyrs in the foam, super labs will mate humans and animals to make Humanzee a new man. These anyway were the thoughts of the Wold Company as we sang to the severed heads, "I think I can, I think I can." We gave injections when those heads slavered and palavered, sang to the injectors spinning: "Rockabye godbey in the test tube, now you'll find out how a man makes god." Sling another round of viscose into them. Mouse/viscouse.

Sensory experiments enhanced a man's nose who could now chat with a devil and smell like a dog. Ancient DNA's revived to join the crew underground, which in Latin means subvert or turn from below. Trillions of brain cells came online so the present man-god could prevent this tragedy of not building god. Crimes against the mouse, murine (mouse) hybridomas, hybrid cell lines that create Monoclonal antibody therapies for treatment of human disease, were long old hat, like replacing herbs with microbial transformation. Level 1 stuff, loss leaders, Trojan Horses, gimmes. After you have sacrificed millions and millions of mice, and raised your sights to Pig-Man fluorescent cats and dogs and spider-goats, rabbits don't seem much, or cows experimented on, horse) because the one overriding purpose preoccupies, "a mindset and attitude so different from the average human that they may as well be a separate species. Order and chaos, yes and no, but wiping out the mouse would be a tragedy.

So the human is the obvious second goat. "Second Life" Bio vanity science in the labs. Personal, social disintegration underlay experiments without a cause. Conscienceless, millions and millions of beings sacrificed so human life supersedes. This singularity was the HYBRID AGE, human organs grown in pigs and dinosaurs reconstituted from 80 million year old DNA stored in their bones. Considered fantasy to the culture above, below, a serious effort of government and business remade dinosaurs and paired all kinds of human and animal genes for human Zorse beings, Not Beings Plus, enhanced, parading nanobots…. 'practice of Nym....'"I sometimes feel that what I have become has transcended a fundamental boundary of propriety and is setting an absolute standard." This "sustaining a self-formulated identity" is capable of deceit.

Crypto embryology was all the rage, cryptozoologically cloned to join with those extinct. Clinics for chimeras, hydras, minotaurs, all ethical of course, offered the endangered a better life. Super science, literature and philosophy led, but business and government were hard behind. It was a Noah's flood of making monstrous when the super collider on line alerted something was up, "some kind of invasion of spontaneously swelling and shrinking spherical or wheel-shaped creatures" had already occurred. Trains lined up busier than usual those nights. We needed ear plugs to stand the roars, and goggles, for these were not Ezekiel's cogs even if they so appeared:

"They were identical wheels, sparkling like diamonds in the sun. It looked like they were wheels within wheels," Dr Bertolucci later confirmed. He said there would be an "open door," at the LHC but they would only be able to keep it open "a very tiny lapse of time, 10-26 seconds. Super Collider –Clunker Statue, Level Four

Nanobots with tweezers lined up to catch the strays "Getting in and out or sending something in" (November 2009), the good news from France was another hole in the faerie wall! Faerie faerie on the wall, where's the biggest hole of all?

Yours truly on the Level, De Kurk Wold.

Space Alien Politics. Phil Schneider In Country

Here's what General MacArthur told the West Point cadets: "We speak in strange terms, of harnessing cosmic energy, of ultimate conflict between a united human race and the sinister forces of some other planetary galaxy. The nations of the world will have to unite, for the next war will be an interplanetary war" (October 8, 1955, also 12 May 1962). The nations of the world, he might have said, must unite against the Buggers! **According to Phil Schneider**, who constructed many underground bases to defend against such forces, every year of the known "white world" contains forty-four years of research and development in the "black." The "Alien Agenda" out of this calculation enabled defense contractors to make 2,816 years progress in black weapons and advanced aerospace research in the 64 years from the formation of the CIA in 1947 to 2011. They would have explored the solar system, time traveled, invented anti-gravity and collected

widgets from all over space. Add 2816 to 2011 and you get the year 4827! Subtract and you obtain the present advertised state of our technical age, which compared would equal 795 B.C, just before Homer wrote the *Illiad*. We give some cryptographic exercises here to crack this code, for Schneider has seen Bo Diddley up close, and documented the 131 Deep Underground Military Bases.

If the general thought that "the nations of earth must someday unite against attack by people from other planets" it could be believed the Exocrates would conquer earth by 2029, were that not also the proffered year of Singularity, unless of course the two are the same as Schneider says, and have been lo these years. But why wait when it just gets harder? Something is preventing: Gideon lights in the bush, a lamp, a pitcher, and a trumpet, people singing and praising Yeshua at night? Grant that in the movies ET breaks down the parameters and distracts people so they cannot attend their own demise. They don't look at their chemtrailed skies or irradiated seas. Even if rapture means *shoah* for the world, how likely shall consumers stomach the alien or the Judgment of God who *makes the nations prove*, shall we say, the United States?

Nazi Scientists

A thousand Nazi Paperclip scientists authorized by President Truman infiltrated American science in 1946, bringing special poisons like sarin, Klon B with 9/91, or tabun (they had invented mustard gas before). Then the Pope, Hillary and Barak could pre-announce the creeping of WW III, and the war guys in D.C. benefit Dow. Nazi medical science iced prisoners to death in concentration camp bathtubs to increase underwater survivability in submarines and space. Nazi LSD began the CIA psychology-fracture machine. Rocketry, chemistry, med science, criminality were all sold on Paperclips. The number was up to 1500 by then, and climbing.

George Kennan and Dean Acheson threatened that if we didn't use them the Russians would. The Russians would take the lead in poisons as they had in mind control and ESP, for *there* the Germans were weaker. Pure Nazis were more pure occultists after the Spear of Destiny than applied. They did harness raw Egypt in their underground cities. America learned from the subterranean penal colonies of Nordhausen and the gas chambers, and built the Eagles Nest of Hitler's HQ in space. Intimidation architecture to cow the ***Untermenshen*** sub human classes was made digital in experimental cell towers. Weimar-Millennial Americans would go quietly when their time came. But ***Ubermenschen,*** transhumans imported to the West like the rats with bubonic plague that the Nazis tried to land off the English coast from U-Boats, showed Camp King subjects how to hatch the CIA black programs of Bluebird to get ahead of the curve. Maybe rats, Baal or buggers can swim, but maybe not, so DARPA invented a new aquatic rat for the Beltway. Lesser German endeavors airlifted hoof and mouth disease to England, but were countered by the Allies dropping potato beetles.

Of course Shiva has a third eye and a snake around its neck so expect more spit. And, oops, Shiva has three heads and poison in his throat.

At war, the conscious against the unconscious, hatched many constructs of Hive truth and falsehoods for Diversion. Regulations require Black Science to do what the world calls wisdom stages in its plans for control. If this is fiction, *Enders Game* is the front and *Neon Genesis Evangelion* is the back where earth unites to defeat the good angels to ally with the bad, thus to preserve global culture. Global culture is that delusion held in common by astrophysics, Hawking, Existential Survivalists, NBC and the

Vatican. You can add universities, PhDs, bill collectors. "It's a system of power always deciding in the name of humanity who deserves to be remembered and who forgotten."

To summarize Phil Schneider's last lecture:

Deep Underground Bases judge the aliens not as ETs but HDs (HyperDimensionals) whose horseshoe aircraft were seen in 1909 at Truth or Consequences N.M. After Grey demons appeared in 1933 and 1946 at Ellis AFB, atomic explosions executed at Bikini Atoll were intended to wipe out the Grey underwater base at Bikini Island (Operation Crossroads). All this is in the movie, **Soft Disclosure**.

Schneider worked at building 13 UG bases where he reports 100,000 children and 1 million adults are taken each year (numbers vary). There have been some escapes. Kurk Wold got out. The 131 UGs can convert to prison camps (Richard Sauder). Blue Helmut UN troops would occupy 3 UGs per state with scalene triangles, no side equal to another. Slides go down from the FEMA camps to the levels below, so take some wax paper. All 131 bases, 4 1/2 cubic miles each in expanse, are connected by 2 lane roads and mag-lev trains 5700 feet under ground. The UN built one 30 cubic miles large in Sweden. *Martial law research* training for police is available at each base. Tesla's lab in Colorado Springs connects to large caverns of their local UG.

All this is brought to you by a series of card tricks, poppy, hooey and poo. Demon aliens, Nazi war criminals, Gestapo agents who give "consenting human experiments" to nonconsenting human participants, inhabit eight levels. Black ops at Harvard, depersonalizations at Yale fragment different selves to prepare students for the modern America. These compartments are OK'd at Stanford because students sign consent. There goes Ted K with multiple, daily dunkings by MK Ultra look alikes produce lone gunmen in theaters, churches, stores and parking lots. Black Water private contractors become clerks, murdering geneticist doctors became pediatricians, Gestapo agents completed CIA training, and paramilitary exterminators got jobs in police. Germ warfare biologists did cancer research of the CDC. Busy thousands founded DARPA, then NASA, and then DISCLOSURE! They were the yeast that blew American white bread up into the bun. British dough was already *superminded*. The American soul, doing what it pleased, found out during the blackout what Bolivians know. Nobody knows the master like the slave. Nazis-prepared infection explored outer space. Epidemics spread tissue metamorphoses within the body. Allo-toxin materialists ruled as Rome. They were inspired Nietzsches, Beyond Truth and Falsehood at DARPA.

As the King of Babylon, shaking arrows out of his quiver, might have said after consulting images and looking into the liver, the real *Wunderwaffe* of weapons of ingenuity came to America and Britain from Germany. Russia got to take the Ark of Gabriel to Antarctica to *Neuschwabenland*, not on record, but the Allies got the antigravity bell that Walther Riedel, Nazi head of V-2 designs, says *made short trips around the moon*. Along with *space mirrors*, early Project Blue Beam runoff stuff, the American *Raubkammer* proved chemical weapons against cats and dogs, horses and cows. Pigs were moved to the Templeton ASU complex for adaptations to the black hole, broken dimensions and ever popular mind controls (see *Operation Paperclip*, 92. Annie Jacobsen). By the time you read this, 1,477 underground bases will have been readied around the world to serve 107,200 prison boxcars of an expected 15 million dissidents for fun, in case they refuse to go.

Schneider disbelieved! He claimed the alien New World Order was a secret force to conquer the world to rule a fascist one-world. At least then we would be safe. Gun control would finally pay off. Schneider claimed that "the alien agenda" is "to kill off up to 7/8 by 2029," but it may take longer, that there are U.S. "black budget projects" in the trillions that "garner one quarter of the entire gross national product of these United States," that "at least 1.023 trillion dollars is used in black budget programs," funded primarily by fgov drug running. That's nothing compared with the 8.5 trillion dollars missing from Pentagon budgets in accounting up to 2013.

While you are looking at your cell phone profound existence is moving. Where is it going? We mix planes one with another as if there were no above and below, merely digital. This is one skin the onion makes, but there are more. Would you take them by force? If there are 140 elements in the periodic table as Schneider says, and hundreds of massive underground cites and bases manned by foreign troops at ready for dissidents, funded by that 8.5 Trillion missing from the Pentagon Budget alone, and if the people are the very *untermenshen* Nazis experimented on and exterminated, which NFL game will you watch? The threnody of Carmarthen, *which one is this, which one is this, ask me I know them* was spoken of graves. In our time things disappear: desaparecidos, tunnels, multi dimensionals. You must add, "Johnny I hardly knew ya" (Irish Song lyric). One day a great surprise promises to be in store. Not the hologram coming down, but the One who shall be seen. "Every eye shall see him" (*Revelation* 1.7).

So for all the remote viewing and insider talk in the navy tubes, says Ron Blackburn, holographic tech, and the Morgan Reynolds' lawsuit, and Clark McClelland, Pilots for truth, April Gallup at the Pentagon, the Maxwell air force base holograph, Gravitational Force of the Sun: Pari Spolter, Henry Deacon's life on the planets, the Branton Files, Clifford Stone, NASA *'secret' astronaut corps, John Grace's OH Krill Paper,* Miles Johnson on the Bases Project, John Lear on 9/11,-- there is not one word of the angels that so outnumbered Sennacherib's men in their camp (Isaiah 37.36; 2 Kings 6). And what of the fate of the King of Babylon (Isaiah 14), the King of Tyre (Ezekiel 28), and Pharaoh, that great dragon that lies in the midst of his rivers, who says, *My river is my own; I have made it of myself.* Nebuchadnezzar was looking over Babylon and said, *I will exalt myself,* "but the fish of the rivers will stick to the dragon's scales" *(Ezekiel 29).* So while one could say that Nazis look alikes at NASA, DARPA and CERN are worries, even if these beings push the switches and open the doors, we can't say there is *no* difference between the greys, the Nazi war chemists and the pasty NASA Nazis (John Lear), no difference except the propaganda. Who seduced the American/British to convert tabun and prepare their psycho war? If you were in America the bad guy was abroad. They were afraid of the greys, but not of Yahweh!

Underground Archuleta. Schneider's Death.

Two days after **Phil Schneider's death** from a surgical rubber tube that caught in his neck Detective Harris dispatched the body to a Funeral Home without a coroner's exam. We have a dearth of sudden autopsies. Ask about the Justice Scalia's. The medical examiner-- "Dr. Gunson made no mention of the metal plate in his head, or that his right lung had been removed when he declared the cause of death to be "strangulation by ligature asphyxiation." It was "suicide," almost as if it were the body of Prince Philip. Phil Schneider is one of many conspiracy nuts to go up in smoke, amid incredible claims to *auto de fe*--**Paul Bennewitz, Danny Casolaro, William Cooper, Jim Keith**. Shipped to pre-existing "FEMA camps" funded by Reagan's Rex 84 Project, Project Garden Plot and Operation Cable Splicer, offered advanced placement for those allocated to be *"Saved From the End of the World."* Google it my friend at the *Camel Saloon*. Along the Jersey Turnpike Schneider's timetable of the public dream of white science, vaccines, internal combustion engines and liquid fuel rockets mans the toll booths. The Last of Schneider's texts at the Preparedness Expo of 1995-- Exogenous Underground Bases, FEMA camps and Chemtrails --under the heading of "Byzantine Hybridomas", were secret "Black Ops" of Military, FBI and rogue elements pertaining to the under-government. These include "about 6 million to 7 million human beings slaughtered by the aliens at this present time," huge vats containing alien and human body parts floating in the plasma of ensanguinated cattle and Sherry Shriner.

Mass Narcosis

Under the influence of mass narcosis opiates and hallucinogens when good substitutes to numb brain cells fail, induced deterioration masks recognized diseases like the effects of lithium, aluminum and barium that induce Lethargy. Thirst. Stomach distress. Sudden Weight gain. Muscle/joint pain. Twitching, can't taste your food, slurred speech, blurred vision. Confusion, hallucinations. Impotence. Kidney pain. Hair loss. Gofernment corporations spray both for debilitation and market the antidote. Science has an epidemic of ADHD and autism, especially mercury in vaccines. What's the drug that produces indifference to flu shots? Stay tuned for the President. Lithium desiccation is useful in increasing conductivity for psychoactive/social ongoing tests. Dispersal plumes affecting human beings and the natural environment from laboratory applied pathogens correlate with electromagnetic frequencies! The proper term is geoengineering. Your Google wants you to write reengineering. Beneath the soil of the Superfund, considered strip mines, polluted rivers, forest fires of days gone by, no citizen is alerted to the attack on American *soil* by the aluminum, lithium, and barium morning glory clouds of water, air and soil. Lithium spraying, lithium carbonate, mood stabilizing bipolar mania glaze a fine tremor nausea headache over hyperthyroid increase weight gain and ataxia gait. These are Lithium benefits: lithium chelates aluminum! Monsanto has got a seed that grows in the new aluminum soil. Wm. Burroughs had bad dreams of this reality. He kept guns in his bread.

Loss of Conscience

The "government of the People, by the People, for the People" at one time defined your beliefs, no matter how disagreeable, as worth fighting to guarantee. In an inherent contradiction of allegiance, the armed forces swear to defend the Constitution *and* obey the President and appointed officers even as they offend it. The Constitution assumes armies are composed of citizens whose unquestioned allegiance is to their families and their freedoms. This implies a soldier has the responsibility and *right to disobey any order to violate the freedoms of the Constitution*. And when does the soldier realize this? During martial law his conscience tells him so. Ever wonder why officers say when they take the oath of allegiance that it is done without mental reservation or purpose of evasion? American soldiers have turned their guns on many countries. Gofernment assassinates Americans abroad and covertly at home whoever the state deems. But they don't line up to watch as the citizens of eastern Europe did executions at the ditches of the *bullet holocaust*. Americans have Tik Tok for this. Cell phone cameras photograph their loss. The question is not, where is the good, because evil masquerades as good, as all morals about earth, the poor, minorities mask further depravities. The good is the wholesale importation of Nazi physicists, rocket scientists, medical doctors, chemists under the guise of beating Japan, then Russia, then terror. Parallel structures of Nazi colonies in Argentina and Uruguay, not to speak of Antarctica, ignore what morality might have existed. I love a good moral war, don't you? Fast forward fifty years to see the Nazis transhume man say nothing of the science kept out of public sight.

Reporting "facts," the endless rebroadcast and analysis of "facts" Andre Maurois' *Tragedy in France* outlines how Germany possessed the soul of France by manipulating Vichy confederates. Hannah Arendt got in trouble with the Zionists for her report that Jewish leadership was complicit in the deaths. This "evil brainchild of the German Nazis" to manipulate the Jewish Council of Amsterdam, "charged with informing the Jewish constituency of their edicts through its official publication *Het joodsche weekblad*, was originally under the illusion that by negotiations it could save Jews! The Council had to **select who would be sent to die** in work camps and later to the concentration camps in Poland, an effective tool in their destruction." (Snapper, *The Low Countries and the New World(s)*, "Westerbork to Auschwitz," 179).

Why England Slept by JFK shows appeasement in Britain before the war. Why Earth Slept, Tragedy in Earth you can call it, the invention of the alien savior, fabrication myth, propaganda and appeasement can be the title when Shiva has gained status for that statue at CERN, but many arms reach back from 2016 to 1950. **The Nazi makes a good Shiva** for reaching into every American institution of government, education, medicine, physics, psychology. So if Nazis couldn't be on medical school faculties when they were found out they could at least go to university and serve and if not there go into public health. Only as a last resort were they shipped to Argentina with that indispensable dark knowledge. The ones that got to stay worked in public health, if you call CIA experiments in interrogation public, or health. They founded Bluebird, MK Ultra, and in the Iraq interrogations radicalized that nation to protect the homeland, they said. Quoting McNamara, Rusk, Bundy, attacks on American soil sponsored by CIA took comfort at least in that if he's a Nazi at least he's not a Communist.

Of course Shiva has a third eye and a snake around its neck so expect more spit. And, oops, Shiva has three heads and poison in his throat.

Dulce on the Archuleta

Schneider did a deep drill at Dulce N.M. in August 1979, sinking four shafts with lasers and components of the **Tunnel Boring Machine**. When the TBM came up broken Schneider and other geologists went down in a bucket to check. At the bottom, 2-1/2 miles below they met the Grey, later called Bo Diddley. Some think there were no survivors. If you think that stop reading.

The facility at Archuleta occupies the 4-corners area of New Mexico with the highest levels of missing people in the country. **According to Schneider,** women of child-bearing age, and young men from 10 to 15, are the prime age for going missing there,

*Bograming as they say. Schneider discovered an underground amphitheater of large meeting rooms identical to the U.N. with a specific "raised seating area" where seven foot tall Grey DJ Buggers could dictate to U.N. officials without bending. The U.S. Constitution does not apply under ground. Citizens held no legal standing and international leaders are at the mercy of Orson Scot Card. According to Schneider, the Offut AFB, in Nebraska, is home to angel/bugger bodies and their buggies, with long rumored undergrounds at the WPAFB facility in Dayton.

Finally however, there is a defense for those who can point down that uric power of the stars as Edward Abbey first proved at his sighting Grand Canyon with such precipitation. He said, "the first thing I did was urinate off the rim onto a little aspen." (*One Life at a Time Please*, 124). **Phil Schneider's research** along these line proves that what is noxious to the aspen works on the infamous *les Petits-Gris*. Phil conducted this tactic out of the worst part of the mythical politic attached to FEMA above. Those bases he innocently rappelled down were filled with Archuleta's *Eisenaliens, or *iron lions*. This was Schneider's worst trouble until the rubber tubing, but surely no more so than the rest of us. As his wife has reported, when the battle of Archuleta was all but lost, and he had sustained such injuries that *his body was covered with "shrapnel" wounds (about 500), and he had burns and skin grafts and missing fingers and his private part was cut right down the center and part of his ear was replaced and he had a metal plate in his head and part of a lung* -- "he peed in his hard hat and threw the pee at the aliens and killed some of them. Many years later in a fictional program on TV the aliens, still highly allergic to ammonia, would die of it." Now do you know what to do?

Note: *fgov* is an abbreviation for gofernment.

<u>**Pat Simonelli**</u>

To the Fez reader who has never listened to Art Bell or George Noory on Coast to Coast AM, Phil Schneider's Dulce claim is a good starting point in the world of strange tales.

.

Satan at the Super Collider

This was *the damned worm who pierces through the world*. CERN, the European Organization for Nuclear Research, and its objectives are viewed through the vision of Satan given by Dante in Canto 34 of the *Inferno*. The climax of this descent into dark matter is foreseen, along with the extra dimensions, parallel universes, black holes to open doors to other space/time dimensions. CERN's stated purpose in France/Switzerland, where

> the side on which he fell from heaven;
> for fear of him, the land that once loomed here
> made of the sea a veil and rose into
> our hemisphere; and that land which appears
> upon this side--perhaps to flee from him--
> left here this hollow space, and hurried upward. (121-26)

We walk past monuments erected by our selves and pretend they are something else, as if, like the shag carpet Dante climbs down to pass through hell they are a foothold in the underneath, anything but what they are. It is the frozen visage of Satan down which he descends, climbing down Satan's shaggy sides and between the tangled hair and its ice crust past the point where the thigh begins. To land this way Satan must have been cast head first into the earth's center and stuck there, a kind of jack knife in two dimensions but in three a somersault reversal of gravity, immobilized in ice, for his fall displaced all the land, pushed it into the northern hemisphere. In two dimensions a v and inverted v from entrance and exit collapsed together. They are collided to free the energy, in this case Satan, CERN's drunken purpose, prematurely we should say, as if that were possible, but actually before the fact of Satan's incarceration, since that comes later in earth's time, after most of these matters are resolved. Then he is not frozen, but chained, then released, then cast in a lake of fire.

Satan is *a sort of structure* (7) *so towered from the ice, up from midchest* (29) *two wings spread out* (46). *Do you still believe you are north of the center* (107), *beneath the hemisphere opposing* (112f)? *Descended, down from tuft to tuft, / between the tangled hair and icy crusts* (74-5). Do we really need to spell out the parallels with the *worm who pierces through the world?* When would you believe? No, "that soul up there [consumed head first in Satan's mouth] who has to suffer more...his head inside, he jerks his legs without" (61-3) is a perfect patsy of...fill in the blank. We could stop to look at it a while, except maybe we realize there are other frozen statues there and run.

Literature gives a much clearer view than science but is not believed. And if this is merely Dante being told by (the fictional) Virgil, truly one of the great foreknowings, it remains to divulge the ultimate vision of foretelling, which (the real) archangel Gabriel gives to Daniel, except this is mathematically precise. The 69 weeks from the beginning of the restoration of Jerusalem to the proclamation of the King, that Palm Sunday in Jerusalem, measure exactly, to the day, the time from March 14, 445 B.C. to April 6, 32 A.D. We are in the presence of something so much greater than Dante that it is well worth contemplation if you tire of the same old black hole, time breaking routine that brings the fierce countenance in. If so you can read Scotland Yard's Sir Robert Anderson's, The Coming Prince.

The event of CERN and the cracking of dimensions is popularly interpreted as the opening of the fifth seal of the Revelation and the star Wormwood crashing into the bottomless pit, where alien life expected by advocates and dissenters comes not from the stars but from below. To open a door to these other dimensions in the presence of metaphors of destruction does not hide much, so Shiva's statute at the facility flaunts destruction in the face of the world, dancing destruction, a pun on Oppenheimer's statement that he had become the destroyer of worlds after the first atomic bomb. It goes nicely with the image of broken time, that is of Kali, Shiva's counterpart, projected on the Empire State Building. Saint-Genis-Pouilly, the town of the super collider, is a shrine named after the Roman city which took its name from the Latin Appolliacum, that is, Apollyon, Pouilly, meaning destroyer. Apollo is cited in Revelation 9/11 as apoliea, "whose name in the Hebrew tongue is Abaddon, but in the Greek tongue hath his name Apollyon, king of the locusts who had a king over them, which is the angel of the bottomless pit." These trees make a row. Kali, Shiva, Apollyon, Oppenheimer. At least tit for tat, religion opposing religion, Christian vs. pagan, the clearest statement of this new physics and its exploration of new dimensions of super symmetry might be that it seeks to open the door to the disembodied spirits of the dead, removed spirits trapped in a parallel dimension of the ether world. That this entire technology of the super collider is so inspired does not exactly fit the paradigm that they are dead, but loosed, they loose themselves with this technology.

I know nothing of the world and its stratagems, time and its breaking. In a series of ritual desecrations to unleash the said, Madonna's Rebel Heart Tour "https://www.youtube.com/watch?v=5iUsjWveN2U" G. Ervana) plays D.C., Philadelphia, New York, the same cities and at the same time as Pope Francis. Continuing that same imagery of Crossing Over, breaking dimensions, the Tomorrowland festival immediately follows in Atlanta. This coincides with the announcement at CERN of its highest power disruption of the boundaries between the planes at that same time. That everything is peaceful afterward admirably suits the calm and beauty of that first September 11 morning.

How does Satan break dimensions? The whole cloning program and hybridization of the human genome. How does Satan break time? By attempting its assassination through geoengineering, counterfeiting always by saying that these things are done to save the earth, lessen warming, save humanity, give long life and health. Extra dimensions mean the unloosing of cohorts imprisoned there. All this is done by psychological mirroring too, the practice of imitation of the movements preceding to fake rapport in order to destroy. Was there a Messiah? There will be an imitation Messiah mirrored.

The one smoking gun in all this is the prima facie evidence of the explosion of technology after WWII with a concomitant black shelving of it so we don't really know what it is. This fuels the question of alien technology except that has no smoking gun at all. Where did it come from, the internet proposing earth into a stage one civilization, the mind of DARPA (Defense Advanced Research Projects Agency, part of US Defense Department) , government scientists? The decoding of the human genome? The lab techniques of chimeras? Those drones are not capable of much beyond following orders. They make us think of Hannah Arendt's clerks who follow orders and assassinate the world. The little grey men who presumably showed the Nazis anti-gravity in 1938 showed them also how to clone? Chip and clone become the ultimate measure of DARPA success, chip, clone and kill anybody who can build another system, or anybody who had built the present system, in order to keep it covert. See all the suicide computer scientists of Britain, all the missing microbiologists. So zero energy and anti-gravity got black shelved while the gov built hundreds of underground cities to outlast the wrath of God. If that sounds stringent, it has become acceptable to cite every other deity but the One true, and to mock real judgment with another celebrated by the Shiva destroyer at CERN, built at the ancient site of the temple of Apolloyon destroyer at Saint Genis Pouilly, with the words of Oppenheimer about the atom bomb, embossed in gold on the outer shell, I am become destroyer of worlds.

Now if the Disclosure that this information all stems from Andromeda, Cassiopeia and Sirius seems too much, and if you have not made fifth level contact with the orbs, which is the worst idea since taking DMT, then what aliens are we talking about? The news is at least indigenous. The angel alien fallen who impersonate every light and dark philosophy from science to Tomorrowland, that fell with the chief musician of heaven and think their day has come, and as far as that goes they are right, it will be short. Eisenhower met with them impersonating the greys and so it goes. We face such an amazing mixture of science and myth that they don't make sense without each other. Here one hand we face a myth where unbelievably the U.S. president Obama is to become a stand-in of Osiris and on the other that fallen angels made a technology and gave it to the global junta they created in order to.... And how any of this could be conceived or construed believably makes it necessary to believe that the U.S. president is a clone, following the orders of his controllers, whoever and wherever they be. There is no nice way to say that presidents, prime ministers, chancellors have been cloned since Jimmy Carter. Nobody could ever believe that LBJ was cloned, but there it stops.

The other important mixture of science and myth involves the Iraq War II where the alleged covert purpose was to steal the technology from the Iraq Museum that Nimrod and/or Gilgamesh used in building the Tower of Babel, which was not a building exactly, more of an antenna that broadcast the EM frequencies we call scalar and were an attempt to "take" the heaven, whatever that could mean. Of course what it means is destroy the heaven, break the dimensions. The attempt failed because of outside interference, so called, which is one way of saying that the technology was good. What exactly it was of course was the purpose of its theft by the U.S. c. April 8, 2003. The best guess is that it represents a parallel track to the supercollider at CERN to break time, break the dimensions, find dark matter, let loose the hordes, in other words. When technology sounds like myth and myth like technology the simplistic principles of empirical science are out of date. All kinds of alternatives to fallen technology exist, especially Disclosure, assigning these discoveries to infiltrators from Sirius, Cassiopeia, Andromeda. And none of these explain parallel phenomena such as the buried super cites on the sea floor off of Japan at Yonaguni Jima, sunk in toto, more engineering projects of the builders of Babel. Those busy builders!

I began to revisit the reopening of the multidimensional gates located everywhere from Sedona to Bolivia when I became aware that that is exactly what CERN seeks to do in this present run, to force open whatever tissue of glue, gravity, veil stands between what they believe is this dimension and the other, serial dimensions of dark matter they think they are measuring, but can't see. The overt religious fervor of this in the statue at the facility, the odd reports of paranormal effects reported around it, the opera Dance of Destruction, filmed to celebrate this run, with its creepy effects, break dancing taken from My Pet Goat II and the applause on all the CERN videos whenever they complete a run, like a moonshot, factor taking the subject as the Days of Noah as an explanation, you know, when people were eating and drinking and giving in marriage right up until the rains came. Shiva the destroyer is a pun on the rains, in this case the doors opening, the gates thinning, to result in, and now here the effects might be a wee speculate, the coming of giants to eat you, the rising from the bed of the Euphrates of the horsemen of Revelation and the seven seals. This last quickly exhausts the viewer.

Back then to reality, or what we call alternative reality, comes the purpose for the Iraq War, which, all other causes notwithstanding, was to retrieve from the Museum of Iraq artifacts Saddam had dug up, and which the American special forces retrieved on the first day of the war, these constituting DNA formulas of Nimrod, to study how he, "began to become," a necessity for transhumans who wish the same upon themselves and must be considered another arm of the destroying Shiva at CERN. This explains why the Americans allowed the looting of the museum after, to cover their tracks. But Shiva has five or six arms. The other booty, flown out by helicopter by night, selected by the American ambassador who was on site to see to it, was, and you will appreciate how this is the counterpart to CERN, the control mechanism and power source of the Tower of Babel, viz. the technology of the fallen angels. That there is a theology anthropology behind all this you can ferret out yourself in the sources of Tom Horn and Steve Quayle and their associates. This bit about the Curator of the Iraq Museum comes 47.15-55.39f in their On the Path of the Immortals "

Allied to this in some odd way, the interview of Alex Jones with Louis Lefebvre about Pet Goat II argues that this is throwing the illuminati imagery back in the face of the elites to cause consciousness, but consider whether it doesn't do the opposite, merely to confirm those images by using them. Any pub is good pub. These are very like those images of Tomorrow Land in Rio and that to come in Atlanta, which pose as initiatory rites to invoke multidimensionals through the portal, so also allied to CERN, presumably to be announced on CNN. The coming cannibalism of the giants to be let loose, "the land devours its inhabitants" (*Numbers*) should be viewed as even more mental and spiritual than it will be physical devouring. If you wonder at all these precursors to the events to come, what they call predictive programming, it is arguably a technique of propaganda to preprogram a reserve data drop before the effect, so that it mimics precognition, or foretelling, and is recognized and therefore more readily triggers belief in that section of the brain where these lodge.

So Bush-Obama Amer-uca, land of the feathered serpent, learns to jump space through orbs with ancient portal technology stolen from Saddam at the same time as CERN does, but with suspicion that there are colliders in the US anyway. You just have to look underground. Good luck with that, as much as even getting onto the Bradshaw Ranch, the Sedona Portal, since it is now owned by the Gov. I say I began to revisit this some years ago because Gilgamesh crept into work on ThoughtGottens and Oracle Binding, which queried, began the first awareness of the Lapis box that was said to be recovered of these remains. Which is left of these remains in the USDA labs on the Beltway we can't find, or the number of these portals yet, but Mount Graham and the Four Corners in addition to Sedona are being bought up. Of course Dulce on the Archuleta is already in the portfolio. Today you can hear about Donald Trump, civil and financial unrest and immigration and receive that there is a higher and lower sort, that immigration coming in to those ports. Well that's what it means to be eating and drinking right up until the flood comes.

Another arm of this Shiva opening portals would be the Vatican offering homes to the space brothers they conjure from de Chardin on to their portal on Mt. Graham, which was brought to us by Senator John McCain. Another portal, but also one masked, or one to mask the work at CERN and at the D. C. government labs with Babel. I almost said Beelzebub. Check the astrobiology here at Baptized Martians, which of course is a joke since, if they have not fallen into sin, as the Vatican suspects, they will baptize us. Then they will kill us. CERN is the consequence of the Vril Society under its occult names. Further research, try dinosaurs at Sedona, suicides at CERN. Fallen seraphim reptilian giants need to be fed.

The best news received in the interim is that we are all in a medieval, Roman system of two classes of rulers and peasants. It is so comforting to be a restored peasant after suffering the illusion so long that I was better, something else. My aunt insisted always from an early age that we are all peasants. I have come home to it, knowing that I know nothing of the world and its stratagems, time and its breaking, even if I sue the words, and that I am so unimportant that I can be left alone to live my illusions without interference. It was my own fault for ever thinking otherwise, but we also recognize that is the programming put upon us at birth, in schools, in society, that we matter and that we can do anything. All illusion, all chimera. There are two reigning possibilities, ET vs the Nephilim, with many permutations, but the best is the simplest, that they are the same, not that the numbers of intelligent parties who have had experience of ET would accept this. Steve Greer had early experience of contact. It became his *raison d'être*, his reason for being, leant significance to his life, although he is a member of the ruling class and not a peasant, which should give pause.

Two classes of ET emerge, the android manufacture, programmed life form, chipped and cloned (extended to most Hollywood stars) and the "real" kind that say they are from Andromeda or Sirius and come with benign intent, little Speilbergs, for whom we must enter an age of peace, not war, so earth can have more generations, another neat bifurcation between the real and the unreal to draw participants toward the middle. Even though the Hegelian is decried by all these groups they all use it. The Disclosure effort by all accounts is to come public in an alien war, etc. a false flag event run by the rulers to consolidate ever more power. Before this all gets lost in the details, these appearances of occupy the black budget, black shelved, sequestered technologies that have been known to be thousands of years ahead of what is used on the earth, from little greys for the Nazis, etc., who can take many shapes. It is pertinent that *Revelation* says that this was the beast that was, that is not, then that is and then that is no more, that this somehow explains a timeline that repeats the days of Noah, for there is plenty of history in ancient times of these entrances into human affairs, making fit extensions of themselves, i.e. hybrids, giants. In this there seem to be three: the first who fell, their breeding of a hybrid race, and further breeding into giants.

Diffused and disguised effects are to be argued from all of this, that is, radiations, skips and jumps in different directions affecting crime, war, earthquakes, politics, social movements (refugees, chemical plant explosions, Santiago, Chile, bogus nuclear treaties, Hajj stampede, threats of N and S Korea, China, Russia, the all purpose Obama dignitaries and the Pope). It was part of this world illusion that its best and brightest had all done unspeakable things and made bargains to display their beauty and power that made them so shine, but which in actual fact had debased them so far beneath the idea even of a human that they retained only the vestige.

Cited. *The Inferno of Dante Alighieri*. Allen Mandelbaum. 1980.

Melt

This happens in one week, 11 Feb to 18 2016: the Pope arrives in Mexico, 12 Feb. and Scalia is killed. The Grand Mosque Caliphate had contacted Russian Patriarch Kirill for *Instructions given to Muhammad* to process the Ark of Gabriel. Following the Havana Joint Declaration of Pope Francis and Patriarch Kirill declares at Holy Trinity church in Antarctica,"the whole world *below*." Rampant supernaturalisms, borderline intelligence down in Antarctica. World elites resettle New Zealand. Cyclop lit, pre-Adam tech, Obama visits and bigwigs flee the Russian hack. They bury a masonry grid, dig it up to proclaim the alien <u>here</u>

Antarctic Timeline 2016

The Pope arrived in <u>Mexico 12 Feb 2016</u> after his visit to Cuba to meet the Russian Orthodox Patriarch Kirill. He left Mexico late on 17 Feb from Juarez, right across the border from El Paso where Scalia's body was taken 2/13, after his death. Just leaving, he would say **in midair** that <u>Donald Trump was not a Christian</u>, but on 2/12 the deep net had Trump telling Putin in a hand delivered note that they better never meet in Texas if they expected to live. This was a reference to the Bush/Texas/Dallas/assassinations, but by the evening of the 12th Scalia was dead. On 2/11 these same intelligence sources say Obama met with Scalia at the Cibolo Ranch, where Scalia had gone with the Bohemian Grove hunting club (St. Hubertus) of which he was (or not) a member, gratis of Obama's Poindexter. On Feb 9, 2016, four days before the death of Scalia, a Podesta email read, "don't think wet works meant pool parties at the [Cibolo] Vineyard."

Pick up the trail of a timeline from 11 Feb to 18 2016, the same week of the death of Justice Scalia, staged to look suspicious with a pillow over his head. That most culpable pillow on his face was a symbol of smothered speech and thought. If coming disclosures lift their pillows and dazzle us with the staging the news will be complete with the usual defamiliarization of reality. Blended undistinguishable narrative voices will so stultify with structural disorder and abstraction it will compel belief. The roster that week led off with Justice Scalia, Pope Francis, Russian Patriarch Kirill and Donald Trump, and continued early and late with John Kerry, Newt Gingrich, Vladimir Putin, Barack Obama, James Clapper, Buzz Aldrin and a whole host of players from the Russian Baltic Fleet of 2017, but extending back to the President of the Republic of Chile, Sebastian Pinera Echenique, Presidents of Uruguay and Ecuador, 2/2/13, King Carlos of Spain and Prince Harry.

We are programmed to accept leaks as "chatter" that intelligence uses to find terrorists, but such judgments are really cabalistic. Elites love numbers, letters and signs. Hence, these events occur in a leap-year, right before the beginning of the calendrical American election cycle (always a leap year), celebrated 29 Feb. Secretary of State Kerry's flight to Antarctic the eve of the American election, 2016 serves these ends. The **7.8 NZ earthquake** the last night of his stay, two minutes after midnight, 14 November 2016, recalls a prior "earthquake," not exactly reported so, that was the deep state motive for the Pope meeting the Russian Patriarch in Cuba in the first place. Those offices were convening for the first time in a thousand years, similar to the thousand year span breached in the *Instructions* for **the discovery of the Ark of Gabriel**. Excavations under the Grand Mosque in Mecca, September 2015 caused two major disasters, 12 Sept and 24 Sept 2015, which "quakes," called lightning (plasma emissions) in the chatter, motivate the meeting of **Pope Francis and Patriarch Kirill** in Cuba.

 The Grand Mosque Caliphate had contacted Patriarch Kirill in Fall 2015 because his Russian Orthodox church retained a copy of an ancient ms. (c. 1050) called *"Gabriel's Instructions To Muhammad"* about how to "handle" the Ark. The *Instructions* presume to have enabled the Ark's excavation according to protocol. Why the Ark should then be transported to Antarctica is not obvious unless some notion of the disclosure-discovery ruse is taken, and further that technology being collected all over the world was also being taken there. The Russian Orthodox Patriarch Kirill had a Russian historical connect with the Mosque generally. This produced the order by President Putin for a fleet of *Russian ships* to transport the Ark **6 Dec 2015** to Antarctica. Immediately following his meeting with the Pope in Cuba in Feb 2016 therefore, when Patriarch Kirill flew to Antarctica **18 Feb,** the Ark had already arrived. Intelligence sources further say that in Cuba the Pope had given his own **secret ritual ms**. from the Vatican archives to the Patriarch to be performed in Antarctica. The *Book of Enoch* is a probable context for this. When those factions and Kirill with the ms. rendezvoused in Antarctic **18 Feb** 2016 to "repatriate" the Ark, those events of Feb 2016 were punctuated by the Pope declaring Trump cannot be a Christian (**18 Feb**), drawing him as a sort of Scalia parody into the mix.

Antarctica is called "the bottom of the planet." That is presumably why the UN flag is centered on the *North* pole. North is "up." It is the supposed top. Europe is up. Patriarch Kirill's suggestion that the **Antarctic is** *the summit of the planet with the whole world below* is upside down to the European-UN design. From the South the oceans are seen as in Plato's *Timaeus* with the continents encircling them. This new presumed "unity of the earth" of a *one world* continent that rings Ocean is why Patriarch Kirill is in Antarctica in the first place, the least intuitive place for a Russian Orthodox Patriarch. *One ring to rule them all.* If trading the UN for ET sounds like jumping from the frying pan into the fire, the Patriarch offers no better explanation himself than the series of circumstances around the **Ark of Gabriel.**

The *Instructions given to Muhammad* by the Angel Gabriel in a cave on Mount Hira, (610 AD) near Mecca were Muhammad's First Revelation entrusted to his care with the proviso that this "box/ark" of "immense power" was forbidden to use as it belonged to God only and was to be buried until its future uncovering in the "*Day of the Resurrection.*" This shrine was the "*place of worship the Angels used before the creation of man.*"

The **Joint Declaration of Pope Francis and Patriarch Kirill of Moscow** from Cuba said that "human civilization has entered into a period of epochal change...the international community must undertake every possible effort to end terrorism through common, joint and coordinated action. We call on all the countries involved in the struggle against **terrorism to responsible** and prudent action... and **not permit a new world war.**" This relic of angels before the creation of man was to be unopened, but **they opened it**, and now wanted to put it back. The *"ancient secret manuscript"* given to Patriarch Kirill by Pope Francis, presumed written directly by the *"watchers,"* that is those same angels described in the *Book of Enoch,* was for this purpose.

We cannot fail to mention by comparison how the supernatural tenor of angels and rituals belongs also to the Third Secret of Fatima that backgrounds the WWIII of the Joint Declaration. After talk like that literally anything could happen in the immensity, "a Bishop dressed in White 'we had the impression that it was the Holy Father.' Others... going up a steep mountain... a big city half in ruins and half trembling with halting step... *having reached the top of the mountain, on his knees at the foot of the big Cross he was killed* [with the others]. *Beneath the two arms of the Cross there were two Angels each with a crystal aspersorium in his hand, in which they gathered up the blood of the Martyrs and with it sprinkled the souls that were making their way to God.* **"An Angel** with a flaming sword in his left hand; flashing, pointing to the earth with his right hand, cried out in a loud voice: 'Penance, Penance, Penance!"

Truthers hold that the Ark placed under the pyramids acts like a capacitor in the commentaries of Giza to fractalize DNA sprays out the top to rebuild/re-create the earth. President Putin, who had been first informed about this Gabriel Ark 27 September 2015 ordered bombing of the Islamic State on 30 September 2015, defending Syria, which ceased as suddenly as it began, 14 March 2016, signifying some extraordinary connection to these events in the time frame.

After the service at the Holy Trinity church in Antarctica Patriarch Kirill referred to Antarctica as the summit of the world. Who would have guessed he would echo H. P. Lovecraft who said that the stone towers that brooded there were **"Corona Mundi...Roof of the World"** (43): "Remember you are on the **summit of the planet.** When I blessed water today ...when we bless water we attract this divine energy [which] penetrates through it as we sprinkle ourselves with WATER. WE BLESS OURSELVES as we drink and ARE charged with the union of things physical and earthly with things divine."

Let's Do the Time Warp Again.

Any explanation for these events has to wait until the announcements begin. Bigwigs are not done touring the ruins of the ("Blue Avian") **"Builder civilizations."** Biden (2009 a joke, 2016 for real, to "New Zealand"), Buzz Aldrin, Patriarch Kirill, John Kerry, Mark Gibb (R), and Peter Ryder (Indochina Capital, John McCain, Newt Gingrich. From Mar 2016 to the American Election of November **Obama and James Clapper visit Antarctica** c. **23-27 Mar** 2016 (officially Bariloche in Patagonia). Clapper, Director of National Intelligence had just visited Australia, New Zealand the week before, 15 Mar 2016.

The Obama visits suggest the bigwigs were somehow represented there by **Buzz Aldrin** on 1 Dec 2016, perhaps as an unofficial Ambassador to the newly "excavated" preAdamites from his previous contact with them on the moon. **Just after** the visit of the American secretary of state **John Kerry** on the eve of the American election, **Nov 7-11, 2016**, the same day, within hours, India withdrew its 500 and 1000 rupee note (Nov 8) to demonetize. Kerry passed off his visit as environmental inquiry, but it was suggestively an attempted divination of the Ark of Gabriel, which fluctuates from invention to real and back again. Kerry's *answer* from the Oracle about its intervention in the **American election** (and therefore Trump) is inferred the next day when he stayed in Wellington, New Zealand on his return. The **7.8 Kaikoura Earthquake** shook him out of bed two minutes after midnight on **14 Nov** 2016. *That would be a No.* Its 7.8 force overturned the sea floor up 2-3 meters down, which suggests the earthquake at the Grand Mosque's second episode of its uncovering.

More rampant supernaturalism of borderline intelligence reports Scalia's ash was used in a ritual to placate the super computer that governs the stargate agency controlling Antarctic, but viewed in these events heightened by Pizza-Pedo-Gate still aborning these suggest the ritualistic nature of the administering minds of *The Elite Wanton* Boys, although they must be more interested in the blood and fat of the sacrifice than its end in ash. *After* the election, news of the underground civilization began to be leaked. Then came the report of Putin's plan to visit Antarctica Jan 2017. He ended up sending his Baltic fleet instead later in 2017. Of course Lockheed Martin, chief manufacturer of the deep state was hiring in full operation in Antarctica with something approaching a thousand super jobs on the recruiting sheets. The meaning of the Steganographic coding in the images of Antarctica in the Podesta coded emails has yet to be revealed. John Key, New Zealand Prime minister, suddenly resigned 12 Dec 2016 as Fulford Speculates, because he was "directly connected to what is going on at 'The Base' in Antarctica: "John Key knows what is about to happen and he does not want to be at the helm of his country's government when it does." Further data both doubted and confirmed involve the Operation Icebridge Ruins, the 3 pyramids, the buried 14 mile

long structure, the Norway dead reindeer line that intersects the
new Zealand earthquake, and the Wilkesland crater discovered c.
2006, as big as Ohio, not to speak of the Red lights of Pine Island.

Three Blind Mice

Synchronicities of these rounds like three blind mice begin at
different times. The straight line is that the Nazis founded New
Swabia in Antarctica in 1939 in a permafrost of doubt, that their
photographs were doctored with "certain primordial and highly
baffling myth-cycles." The Antarctic had always been supposed
from much earlier maps, **Piri Reis** (1513), to have been once
temperate, without ice. But how did the Nazis miss the pyramids
sticking right up on the coast, especially since they are right in
New Swabia (Maud Land), Station 211, near the ice free
mountains of the Muhlig-Hofmann? One supposes that Secretary
of State **John Kerry went to find out why** the Nazis went there,
and then Buzz Aldrin, "earth envoy to interdimensional
space." Director of American Intel, James Clapper had already
been, and Obama, the Clintons and Eisenhower were not far off at
Bariloche. Oh Greada! Affinity science travels late today.

In this series of non concentric circles the New Zealand
earthquakes, Muriwai Beach, 14 Nov 2016 and the Podesta email
pictures of Antarctica in the Anthony Weiner collection, though
not decoded, make a link with the real effects in Antarctica of
earthquakes at the polar opposite of CERN, in New Zealand. It
would seem as if a bow were drawn with the rim of the bow being
the earth and the CERN arrow earthquake its invisible tip. The line
is deep here because on Kerry's visit after Antarctica, last night in
New Zealand, an earthquake inverted three feet of the ocean floor.
We get a better picture of the unseen revealed at Muriwai Beach,

from H. P. Lovecraft and his "monstrous barrel-shaped fossil of wholly unknown nature... tissue evidently preserved by mineral salts...in furrows between ridges...combs or wings that fold up and spread out like fans...fabled Elder Things...stretched on framework of glandular tubing...minute orifices...at wing tips...objects eight feet long all over. Six foot five-ridged torso 3.5 feet central diameter ...seven-foot membranous wings...flexible arms or tentacles found tightly folded to torso (19-21). These irruptions caused great scientific mention, yes? No, the subject was dropped. If you want to see what they saw, whoever they are, start at Invercargill and head south.

 World elites resettling there in New Zealand (89,000 millionaires and counting), fleeing on the barge of their own destruction, flee instead toward it. They just don't know what's coming up. Isais says that their covenant with the scourge that it should pass and not come near to them shall be annulled (*Isaiah* 28.15f). Their fathers toured the Greco-Roman ruins while they traveled to Peru and Cuzco, the Altiplano and the Amazon, but their children will go to the Antarctic. We have to ask Jonathan Swift to explain a world where the *Apsu are comin' and their tails are in sight.* Reconstitute those yahoos while we are still yet in the way, before all highest and beast authorities say they lied to us, but everybody's human, except **Nobody** will be human any more. Science-religion business will prophet the Apsu and the cuckoo past come back. As **Karl Woolf** says before the fact, "we will completely alter mankind for the next ten thousand years."

If that's too big a bite, spores of new Cyclopean literature will bubble up aliens from Antarctica. Pick and choose whether the pseudo neck and probable south are the ends of the tentacles themselves or need to be applied. Artificial Intelligence needs a binary salt of ash and nano code to encrypt the proper form of elite. Then the quantum comes. At first there will only be five point mounds standing up, but diets that absorb inorganic vegetable life and sushi marine will find legs and charcoal grill the game. Even if they multiply by means of pseudo foot that leads to pseudo head and folded wings, bat more than fish will fly like endless rain across the universe.

This is the Dawning of the Age of Antarctica

The shock and awe in this playbook, as if we were being herded to a conclusion that says we do not live on a planet at all but in a bubble-think and were preceded by eight civilizations, our web-footed friends, those masters who will announce themselves through the mouthpiece of their scientists as the Origin of Species. To be kind, to take their hook and line and not to use the froward word, what a gas.

I saw a man laying down a grid of masonry tiles before tearing them up. I didn't see what was covered, only the covering, as if to say he had buried something before and covered it in order to pretend to rediscover it now. In the context this meant that the entire Antarctic disclosure was a tactical plant, a Piltdown Man to roll out technologies governments had been holding back all along, that otherwise they could not explain without severe contempt heaped upon them. **They blamed it on The Melting** from below. How to roll out the technologies that no one would believe, when you had them all along? Ask Ben Rich of Skunkworks, "anything you can imagine we already know how to do." Simply pretend to discover in the Antarctic Melt time travel, extremes of life extension, anti-grav put there by the "Builder Race," the Apkallu, the ET, the alien, the Anunnaki, the Apsu, you name it, then call "factual" what is patently theatre. What is a fact? Whatever scientific authorities say is a fact. Disclosure means a previously hidden made known.

All this theater is worthy of the high global awards Oscars merit with bait and switch. This way **Nobody** gets blamed for blowing up colonies on the moon, Mars, Pluto (pick your own), blowing up the rings of Saturn or for the elite cooking up split dimensions. Where these things *really* came from is thus not an issue and if they are *really* there, **Nobody** asks. **The real is replaced by the "facts,"** being what you are told, the *real* being another quantum yet beyond the ruse.

 Hand picked teams of archeologists and engineers that reveal these finds are the same ones that prepared them for disclosure, cemented them over and then tore them up. Anybody who does not accept the new fact is not just a conspiracy theorist, but anti-science, for science is no longer a questioning of things, it is a believing of them in the history of censorship and controlling beliefs. Those who do not agree will not be heard when the false beliefs of old science are replaced by the false beliefs of the new. One question, was science ever used to fool you before? Is that the fault of science or because science is a tool of the powers to fool?

So this is the dawning of the age of Antarctica, outer perimeter of the dark flat earth where the fgov fills in the harbor at night with tigre extremes and you get an Apocalypse of Stars. Take your pick colonists, the moon, Dulce or Archuleta. Aliens or gfovernment spell check hard. It is an honor to join our brothers there when bodies thrown into Elisha's tomb land on his bones and are taken up alive (*2Kings* 13.21). Wait while the angel looses its vial. Euphrates dries. The Fig Kings march.

There are more things dreamt in heaven and earth than probability. This meeting of Pope Francis and Precedent Kirill in Havana made *two or more meanings of a word exploit multiple and similar-sounding words*. Let's say both sides invented this. Who says there are two sides? Colonists underground and Plain Folk. No questions ask! Over bold they clearly could not touch it and live. So there's more to Antarctica than sunny beaches and clay courts and hot spring resorts ten thousand miles from Moscow where it's really only possible to talk about the idea of the matter, not specific acts and persons who commit to serving them. All particular cases of these concepts must be rejected, not only because they are unbelievable absolutes but because even so who can bring the offenders to account? Are you going to indict the kings and queens of Inland? Sons will be waking up with cold sweats in their beds. What was he doing in that remote earth.

Home Mortars and .50 Cals

To get the significance of the fanfare about to rule we take the emotional shock and weigh it by approximation against the awesome myriad of clues arbitrarily released into the media. It is the beginning of the thing that will cause men's hearts to fail. One of an ongoing series. After all, if NASA is secretly trying to blow up Saturn and if politics are what **Phil Schneider** says you really can't trust any sources in this investigation. What you gonna do when they tell you about CIA 9/11 and the Hollywood moon landing, the Challenger astronaut hit job, that the moon is hollow? And that's just pillow talk. One hundred fifty scientists will trot out with their tails tied together to tell you there's three hundred mile long space ships in the Rings and under ocean and you're not human anyway but an alien your own self. Them fire rats set loose in the country burn it down.

I charge myself with falsity in the absurd connections and verbal satire brought to all these subjects. The Antarctic is being assembled, flotillas arriving and arrived. Heliports, airports, bases, housing for thousands and ten. It is the camp of a decade. What's the point? The new facts, machines, techniques, processes, the antigrav is to prepare for Stage II Civilization say the emergent awake, the orb ones, the truthers, the disclosers. This present state of knowing will be held in ridicule by the new imperial authority. It is the founding of an empire Rome and Babylon would deplore, to make hearts fail not just from the hundred readjustments of its apostles, but the recreation of a world that once existed before the human. The search for Nephite DNA is looking ahead, all the way to next year.

Always looking to turn a phrase could be said to diminish the gravity of the subject, making fun of it. But the purpose is to demonstrate the laughable nature of facts and threats against a promise that *That soul, though all hell should endeavor to shake, I'll never, no never, no never forsake.* There used to be a maxim of prophecy that a prophet once wrong is always wrong, so with the facts. Many sources consulted here have ultimately disproven themselves. So let us consider them fiction in a nonfiction form. By way of proof of this attitude I got a phone call this morning from a friend who has had trouble reading over the years. First the specialists told her it was macular degeneration, then it was cataracts, both of which were removed, and now Fuchs' distrophy, build up of fluid in back of the eye. Next up is a partial corneal transplant.

 The crowning blow came when this was all blamed on heredity. Being a relation I was called to forewarn. If you can learn from the analogy, a chief vehicle of fiction, that is exactly what is going to happen with Antarctica. **The crowning blow will be genetic**, that we are all alien! Ancient Astronauts! QED. Ca Ching, ca ching, the Wanton Boys know how to scare and make you pay. You'll all be buying home mortars and 50 cals. But the good news is the end is false and the beginning can be cured. Try air, water and exercise. Call me in 30 days.

There used to be a super soldier called Max Spiers, killed now by those he would have exposed, who trained him. He outgrew his controls and matured. Among his last statements are two notions, first, that all the centers of the body can be overthrown except the heart, no doubt because these forces have none in this sense, and second that Earth is maligned as it is because **Earth is already the Jewel of the Universe and the human heart is its brightest light.** That, as far as it goes, is how the human fights against the gods.

Glossary and Notes

--Buzz Aldrin. "The fact is that they (aliens) have ordered us to turn away!" is a (purported) direct quote.

--Earthquakes in new Zealand. Earthquakes in New Zealand: Worldview screenshot of New Zealand, Macquarie Island, Guadalupe Island & Nova Scotia / Nov. 13, 2016.

Fight Against the Gods and *Apocalypse of Stars* are two entries maintained online by Kurk Wold at his SuperNats, or Insight Statutes.

--Rand and Rose Flem-ath. *Atlantis Beneath the Ice*. Bear and Co. 2012.

--Fox tails. This is a reverse Samson whose Elite hero ties the scientists together to burn down the human. Samson tied the fox tails to together to spite the Philistines.

--Greada. 1954 treaty between Eisenhower and the tall Grays. Like the *Other Losses* (James Bacque) dismissed as Conspiracy Theory by eight historians at Wikipedia, Eisenhower imprisoned and starved to death some 800,000 German foot soldiers and civilians behind barbed wire, the *crème de la crème* being imported to NASA.

--Graham Hancock's Egyptian Giza Star-based Religion of 11,600 year old destruction of Atlantis is the axis of the Antarctic expeditions, a great counterfeit with the 100 ton blocks of stone fitted to a T, as if by giants. These giants worshipped the stars, their fathers, meaning the Fallen ingenious at counterfeiting. Hancock says he is working hard to change his life through *Ayahuasca*. So is the underground bases writer, Richard Sauder, living in Ecuador.

--H. P. Lovecraft. *At the Mountains of Madness* (Arkham House, 1936). Modern Library 2005.

--Scalia's death. Autopsy of Scalia's Hat. *Sein und Werden*. Corpus.

--Phil Schneider. Space Alien Politics- Phil Schneider In Country. *Red Fez* 88.

--David Wilcock. Endgame Part II The Antarctic Atlantis. Prose version available.

--Karl Woolf. The bad guy in Clive Cussler's *Atlantis Found* (1999).

Autopsy of Scalia's Hat

Citizens of Marfa feel called upon to give account in the death of Supreme Court Justice Antonin Scalia. The autopsy consists of a thorough examination to determine the 1) cause 2) manner of death and 3) evaluate any disease or injury that may be present.

Marfa Courthouse

But in the absence of that cadaverum, since we don't have the body, we must use the hat. The body itself has been predisposed in a secret will to cremation, so we're never going to see it, an act frowned upon by the traditional Catholic. It does however remove the problem at a later date. This fiat accompli involves not just the hat, but the pillow and the judge's name under Cause. The facts issued in the Case are these. Scalia had been "quail hunting," whatever quail that may be, on a ranch in Big Bend country near Marfa owned by the war hero decorated by Obama, John

Poindexter, but without his federal marshal guard. Scalia was

declared dead, with a pillow on his head, over the phone by Presidio County's most infamous female judge, named Cinderela, who had already ruled an arbitrary suicide in her short term. There was just no one else available, although two others had been tried before Cinderela. Not that they had been warned off, but these judges said they just couldn't come to the Cibolo Ranch, and deferred. Cinderela couldn't come either, however pronounced the Justice dead without seeing the body, which was anyway embalmed the same day. These Causes, ruled death by natural cause, occurred within the day, without autopsy.

Hat

In the studied non reporting of the event and its non investigation with the assumption that all is as it appears in this best of all possible worlds, to autopsy Scalia's hat means to look in and beneath the context and take part in what the citizens of Marfa call his martyrdom to the state. To examine cause, such executions derive also from the foolishness of the victim, which, as a preface to Justice Scalia's taking off, occurred in his aping of the martyr Sir Thomas More in wearing a replica of More's hat at the Obama inaugural in 2013. As cause goes, this showboating and bluster made him vulnerable to become a martyr to the state like Sir Thomas More, who Scalia often spoke of, a man who died to defend a corrupt Church and papacy, and considered by many, including his wife, to be a fool for accepting martyrdom. Saint Thomas gave his life because he refused to sign an oath that disparaged the pope and Henry VIII's marriage to Catherine of Aragon. That is, Scalia, with this bluster, invited martyrdom upon himself. Only in Texas could Justice Scalia become a Thomas More martyr for Obama and be executed (covert) by the state for interference with his beliefs.

We should be glad the body was even found considering the cluster of unexplained disappearances in national parks and cities. The absence of investigative reporting in the quick death and disposal is a symbolic disappearance, of which citizens believe more are coming at a future time. They also believe there is a natural/supernatural covering that protects lives which however can be negated by thoughtless speech and acts. This is obvious and more dire the higher one gets. Such thinking preoccupies the cause of King Arthur's death, not his hat or his table, but his sex life made him vulnerable, obviously so if his illicit Mordred killed him. This causality contrasts with Sir Gawain who receives only a scratch on the neck for one stray veniality. According to cause our past president JFK's amazing and complicit affairs made him vulnerable in ways that allowed his taking, to which our citizens complain that who then wants to be famous if so little an error can get you killed? Everything is magnified in the dry air of the Marfa flats.

Look at David's loss of his sons over his lusts and consider Dr. King. Made moralists agonize over such assignations, proved and unproved. Scalia is called Scalia Santo Subito for the bombast of his head wear. Consider the moral agony of Elizabeth Scalia, no relation, over the murder of last day abortionist George Tiller, worse than Mengele. Levinas gives it best: "Everyone will readily agree that it is of the highest importance to know whether we are not duped by morality." Whether Scalia died to defend a corrupt state and its morality or for blocking crucial corporate and international agendas is wonderfully ambivalent.

Pillow

As to manner of death, when you don't believe the news accounts and take them automatically as a twist of some species of deception, that America really founded ISIS, then your first thought of any traumatic social event is misdirection, as if Scalia were murdered in his sleep, poisoned with one of those CIA ice darts to the chest, which would anyway put him in the running among the most important assassinations of American history with Lincoln and JFK. But as to manner, one of the great symbolic props of all time was his body found with a pillow over its face. Like the great "just add one egg" on the Betty Crocker box that activates the housewife to participate in the baking, the pillow over the face is a symbol to smother the world, that the constitution not be taken literally and read as purposed, but as a series of reinterpretations, hence muffled along with all text, authorship and even readers in the Destruktion of meaning in the controls of the mind forged manacles. The hermeneutics of biblical and constitutional issues combine in his assassination by hive, which means only the one stated point of view. The pillow found over Scalia's face in the manner of his death is meant to symbolize this, but even more so its report by Poindexter. If it strikes you that the hat sits on the head and the pillow was found on the face and that these together are telling yet another story, then this we must refer to the true narrator of these events, that being Cinderella.

Cinderela

Cinderela pronounced Judge Scalia dead by phone. To the people of Marfa, who live in the middle of an area of FEMA camps, railroad tracks and mystery apparitions of light on the Marfa Flats, the name of the judge is telling, as if Little Red Riding Hood were to pronounce the wolf or that Goldilocks himself was calling Poindexter. All kinds of symbol are activated by this. Disappearances on the Flats thrill the lower worlds, as if stone cats envisaged faery heads changing, remolting, remolding images, words themselves. As if whole worlds made solid or infirm to be excavated later in quarries, water at the bottom, strata showing marble, dirt, stones, and underneath caves echo networks of a hundred places, voices. So in that environment what was solid became hollow, empty, vacuous and what not at the finish. Then we begin. Aftermath all. Do not answer. Let them cover your ears, put a pillow on your head, because these are just accounts of the events, none of which are actually true even if they are sworn by all the parties in the non news. Whether indeed Scalia even died is not just uncertain, but a fictional version of the superposition to come.

The Marfa utterance of language, roots and alphabet, is the least spiritual power of the Sons against these fgov pronouncements. (The complete spelling of fgov is goferment.) All are meant to function as contradicting puzzles to provoke one end. That said, do not ask what it is, for both things in predictive programming are true. Scalia was both. Symbol is all. He was declared dead by phone by a woman named Cinderela and embalmed immediately without autopsy and we are supposed to believe him murdered. At the same time it is intended that we have no proof to debate these manners rationally. This allows the next ruse soon. Have the cake and eat it quick. Viva le constitution. Every important news event is staged like the Marfa lights and if one knew, predicted. Both sides of programming are true and false, two sides to the natural cause, a third urged by the only journalist to attend the event, who called for revolution, perhaps peaceful. That would be among the forced middles the Hegelian synthesis provokes with the shouting.

Quantum Superposition Sightings

To grasp the *superimposition of world news upon the facts: if
only in Texas can Justice Scalia be a Thomas More martyr for
Obama, get executed (covert) by the state for the interference of
his beliefs in their plans, then this martyr is both the
superpositional target and its opposite. We hardly know what to
believe of our linearity.

Predictive programming and coordination of Scalia's death
(nondeath), occurs at high levels. The Cibolo Ranch where Scalia
died has a modern runway where three or four jets were parked
that weekend. Take it metaphorically: Ground control to Major
Tom. These planes were stacked above the runway waiting for
Scalia to land. The Pope arrived in Mexico 12 Feb. On the 18th he
was in Juarez, right over the border from El Paso where Scalia's
body was taken on 2/13. Just leaving, he would say in midair that
Donald Trump was not a Christian, but on 2/11 Trump was telling
President Vladimir Putin in a hand delivered note that they better
never meet in Texas if they expected to live. On 2/11 Obama took
a secret meeting with Scalia at the Cibolo Ranch, where Scalia had
been lured by the promise of a free vacation gratis by Poindexter.
All this occurs in a leap-year too, beginning the
calendrical American election cycle always occurring in a leap
year, celebrated after the next week, 29 Feb. Toto symbolico.

Spell it out. The Pope mentioned Trump and his Christianity in
answer to a question from a reporter in midair, as he returned to the
Seven Hills. His five-day trip to Mexico, 12 to 18 February 2016,

ended after celebrating Mass at the U.S. border, at Juarez on Thursday 2/18, just across from where Scalia's body was flown from El Paso 2/13 and just within the week when that same Donald Trump on Friday 2/11) had a note hand delivered to Putin. Trump to Putin: "I can promise you this, I will NEVER hold a meeting with you in Texas, neither one of us might come back. He is referencing JFK killed in Dallas, but not yet Scalia in Cibolo. If Donald Trump in making this statement to Putin intending to be "darkly humorous," less than 24 hours after Putin's receipt of Trump's letter comes the sudden and unexpected predictive programming death of Scalia. But the American blackout on the news was overruled by the European Union Times that reported 2/16 that Scalia had a "Secret Texas Meeting With Obama Just Hours Before His Death."

To quote the story: "A report prepared for the Office of the President (OP) by the Foreign Intelligence Service (SVR) examining the letter sent to President Putin by American billionaire Donald Trump appeared to predict the murder of US Supreme Court Justice Antonin Scalia and suggests that just hours before his death had held a secret meeting with Obama aboard a US Air Force plane heading to a secluded Texas ranch owned by a close personal friend and top campaign donor of America's leader."

"According to this polemics of the report, SVR "assets" reported that on 11 February both President Obama and Justice Scalia were at Joint Base Andrews (JBA) scheduled for two separate US Air Force flights from Andrews Field-the first taking President Obama to Los Angeles, and the second taking Justice Scalia to Marfa Municipal Airport (KMRF) located in the southwestern region of Texas near the Mexican border."

"While President Obama was scheduled to depart on one of the US Air Force's two Boeing VC-25 aircraft (commonly referred to as Air Force One), this report continues, Justice Scalia's flight was scheduled aboard a Gulfstream C-37A-which is the US Air Force's designation for their fleet of the popular Gulfstream V private jet aircraft."

"Just prior to these two US Air Force aircraft departing from Andrews Field, this report notes, SVR "assets" assigned to monitoring top American political and military figures noted a "discrepancy from normal protocol" when Justice Scalia's three US Marshal Services Judicial Security Division (JSD) "protectors/defenders" left the airbase with the "personal protection" of this noted jurist being transferred to the US Secret Service (SS)."

"Upon both President Obama and Justice Scalia's different flights departing from Andrews Field, this report continues detailing; an even greater "discrepancy from normal protocol" was noted by the SVR when they were informed by Aerospace Forces (AF) satellite monitoring personal that US Air Force F-16 fighter aircraft from three different bases (Shaw Air Force Base, Montgomery Field, and Luke Air Force Base) accompanied the entire flights of both the Boeing VC-25 and the Gulfstream C-37A-a level of protection normally only afforded to the US President exclusively."

"As to why the US Air Force provided F-16 fighter aircraft protection to Justice Scalia's flight, this report continues, became even more concerning to the SVR when after the flight landed in Marfa, Texas, this "extreme protective air cover" was maintained until the Gulfstream C-37A departed three hours later and flew to

Los Angeles Air Force Base LAAFB) accompanied by its fighter plane escort-and where at the exact same time the American press covering President Obama began questioning where he was, only to be told that President Obama had been missing due to a late-night, off-the-books dinner with three of Hollywood's elite the White House wouldn't further comment on."

"This SVR report, though, "strongly suggests" that President Obama had, in fact, been aboard the Gulfstream C-37A with Justice Scalia from Andrews Field to Marfa and then further traveled from Texas to Los Angeles on it-which they say is the only conclusion to be reached due to the US Air Force's continuous protection of it."

"In support of this conclusion, this report continues, AF radar and electronic spectrum satellite analysis of Marfa, where the Gulfstream C-37A landed with Justice Scalia and (maybe) President Obama, shows a four vehicle convoy leaving the KMRF airport and traveling to a 12,140 hectare (30,000 acre) estate called the Cibolo Creek Ranch."

The part all these together play in the movement of populations like cattle amid mutual announcements of WWIII regarding Syria, Iran, oil, currency, messiah ben David and the Sabbateans is a public distory.

Postmortem

An evaluation of any present disease or injury may include three worlds, and our story can be told in them all. In the first world it is nonreported and denied. Nothing happened, go to lunch. In the second world Scalia, Obama, the Pope, Donald Trump, and

Putin weave an unbelievable fabric as any of the conspiracies of Hillary, fond of naming in her body count, some of identified below. That she has been left out of the later accounts only shows...well we must wait and see.

The First World patina of art, literature, poetry, work life and culture that we think is valuable is a facade. It is all agency and no principal. The First World of Netflix, HBO and selfies deep in the anesthetized state absolutely assures itself it is the only reality. First worlders believe the news is accurate even as they say they don't believe it. Told otherwise they say they already knew that the JFK lone gunman was not a bullet behind, but Twin Towers terrorism, Sandy Hook Elementary, 7/7 London Bombings, Charlie Hebbdo/San Bernardino with the imminence of private contracted militarized police so utterly stultifies that there is no anger at all in the general population, even if informed about the overwhelming evidence of these hoaxes. This is called the *Defamiliarization of Reality comprised of blended undistinguishable narrative voices, structural disorder, abstraction of memory and disconcerting repetition. The audacity of events detaches the citizen from himself, but one instance justifies the others. If Sandy Hook is a well documented government effort to register and confiscate guns, why anyway do they want to disarm the population? An unbelievable scheme these preliminary events serve? This example, most egregious, involves children, but the good news is that nobody actually died. Try saying "Nobody Died at Sandy Hook" as that website says, that it was a FEMA drill for gun control. Any doubts upon this to first worlders will produce paroxysms of hate as they try to choke the life out of you. The First World doesn't like to hear that its disease or injury is that its stars are devils.

A smaller group, not a competing hive, inhabit a margin between the first and second worlds. They watch YouTube every night to build an algorithm revealing that The Charleston Church shooting and the Oregon Umpqua Community College shooting were symbolic acts with Sandy Hook, shooting first graders to traumatize parents, shooting by a white gunman to traumatize blacks, shooting Christian college students to traumatize Christians.

There is no discussion between the first and second worlds. In the Second World deep reality, manipulated by councils, decrees and wars ahead, Stalin is an English agent and the winner pays all the debts of the loser. Extravagance exceeds itself. The polio cancer vaccine, Antarctica/Atlantis fake moon landings, politicat assassinations, underground cities, submarine bases under Kansas, Blue Beam epigenetics, crisis actors, Bohemian groves, aluminum clouds: angelic princes that fell, metallic aerosolized fiberglass slices of microscopic cross section particles in clouds to fill lungs of nano tubules immersed in molten aluminum, all and more are sponsored by hybrids. Generally the rule must be like Lowell discovering Pluto, what you saw you didn't see and what you didn't see you see. All this is seasoned with the scent of atrocious morality and unbelievability to provoke emotional response. What scenario of events includes the Pope, the President, Poindexter, Putin, Trump and Scalia in one story in the space of a week, just before a leap year about to occur? Raise your hand.

This only smacks of Hollywood and coordination at the highest levels for our deception in case we are ignorant of the cloning since 1938 which takes us to Michael Jackson, and the chirping (chipping) of MKultra stars who can be turned off and on like a

button, not to speak of the unspeakable practices of unnamed
ruling classes. It goes into levels always with another twist, for the
active ingredients are after fallen angels--oops we weren't
supposed to say that till later this year or next's Second World
drama. Smoke and mirrors, bait the bear, ruffians in the pit enjoy.

The Third World exposes the false morality imposed by these two
and holds to none of the facts. All of our lives are organized
around a hidden referent, a Shoah to come, a war now breaking our
ribs for which we have no word. Difficult Freedom, Totality and
Infinity, Otherwise Than Being are all reflections of the
presentiment of holocaust as a limited edition of the future. Nazi
charges of subhuman ape and carrier of germs are amplified to the
useless eaters that British royalty thinks the commoners are.

There is no time in this present which does not live the rest of its
life in vigil, endures its life until death cancels the unjustified
privilege of having so far survived. The present of this past pays
with a tumor of the future that nothing can cover except the return
of Messiah. Even if we stand away in the present, neither the past
and its vertigo or the future that grips at our ribs is different, both
are the same. Past and future inhabit nontime which has no
memory and no prediction except searches for a language
dedicated to the memory of those who died, or will, without
naming. Leave the present nameless, for if it fails to name itself,
why should we help it? It is too eager. We deny it space and we
deny it time. This Destruktion of every mountain and hill of morals
makes low. Morality without empathy places flags, magistrates,
palaces and tempests raging in shipwrecks so the murderer can
sanction the world with a clear conscience.

It's a good thing this is invisible. The most important part of these matters is what we will do when faced with the impossible.

Notes

* Destruktion* *"Everyone will readily agree that it is of the highest importance to know whether we are not duped by morality, to be precise, the deconstruction of every European metaphysic of morality accomplished in Auschwitz became a way for the murderer to see in his victim an optics to sanction murder with a clear conscience."* Emmanuel Levinas, *Otherwise Than Being.*

*Defamiliartization of reality. In this case study of the defamiliar, images of order (meaning chaos) are techniques of the Second World. The primary notion comes from a dissolution of language and syntax (public order and myth) that derive from holocaust. Structural disorder, skewed and deflected perspective, obvious paradox, absurdity, repetition and symbolism defamiliarize and re-order events. An abstraction and rewriting of the memory of ego and alter-ego contest public trauma in an avalanche of sources, referents, relations. This means a deliberate avoidance of the facts to defamiliarize. A painting must undergo a process of estrangement from the viewer to acquire meaning. In the written text intentional confusion, incoherence, chaos, invest an unbounded freedom of interpretation, confusing fiction and reality, imposing an illogic upon history and constant escapism. As Raymond Federman observes, "Unless we constantly question what passes for reality, challenge it, defy it, we will always exist in falseness, in a system of twisted facts and glorified illusions, and we quickly become lobotomized by it" (Catalina Botez, Post-Holocaust Interactions).

*Superposition: In the quantum entanglement of Schrödinger's Scalia the man is simultaneously alive and dead. Yet, when one looks in the box, one sees the man either alive or dead, not both alive and dead. This poses the question of when exactly quantum superposition ends and reality collapses into one possibility or the other. The greatest diversion in this psychology is when you automatically disbelieve the news.

Scalia's Hat, A Postmortem

Beside the pillow, Cinderela the judge, and the embarrassment of reporting in the quick claim death and burial of the judicial, be glad they even found the body at all, but disappearance is coming in a future time, of these elite machinations. We can negate by thoughtless speech and acts the natural/supernatural protection to our lives which is more severe the higher we get. In those legendary days King Arthur's sex acts made him vulnerable. His illicit Mordred killed him, contrasting him to Gawain who receives a scratch on the neck for one venial thought. To regard assassination as deriving from the foolishness of the victim. JFK's complicit affairs made him vulnerable in ways that *allowed* his taking, or to add as a preface to Justice Scalia's taking off that by **aping the martyr** Sir Th More in wearing his hat, showboating at the inaugural this bluster made him vulnerable so that he permits himself to become a martyr to imitate, become a Thomas More for Obama, is executed (covert) by the state for the interference of his beliefs. Participatory sacrifice out of Charles Williams doctrines and C. S. Lewis for Joy Davidson, you say, well who wants to be famous if so little error can get you killed? Everything is magnified at that level, for the Christian especially. Lamar Odom can do what he will as long as he behaves, but as a slave. Deals with Yahweh require everything and more. Look at David's loss of his sons over his lusts, made vulnerable...consider Dr. King. Now Christians and moralists agonize over assassinations, proved and unproved, but Illuminati kill as a means of living, so advantage themselves in the moral envelop. Consider the agony of this **moralist, Elizabeth Scalia**, over the murder of last day abortionist George Tiller, worse than Mengele. Levinas gives it best: "Everyone will readily agree that it is of the highest importance to know whether we are not duped by morality." Whether Scalia died to defend a corrupt state and its morality is wonderfully ambivalent.

These comments on the Justice Department Hat:

" I forced myself to reflect upon the importance of getting our pictures of God sorted out in a previous post by briefly engaging what Justice Scalia said about God and state in Louisiana. It would be easy to say Scalia Santo Subito after his **showboating in**

a St. Thomas More hat *during the Obama*

inaugural if, if we didn't pay attention to his theological language. The theological language neither matches the bombast of the headwear, nor the demands of orthodoxy. Scalia might be talking about the Judeo-Christian God, but he does so in radically inadequate ways." Patheos 6 Jan 16 Artur Rosman

"Scalia ended his talk by considering St. Thomas More, a man

who died to defend a corrupt Church and papacy, and considered
by many, including his wife, to be a fool for
accepting martyrdom. More gave his life because he refused to
sign an oath that disparaged the pope and Henry VIII's marriage
to Catherine of Aragon. Scalia pointed out that Pope Clement XII,
the pope during the time of More, was not one of the
most reputable popes in history. And yet, More saw beyond the
current circumstances and believed in the permanence of the
Church that Jesus established." Pursued by Truth
13 Feb 16 Sr. Theresa Aletheia Noble "Justice Antonin Scalia and
the Foolishness of Christianity"

Current views hold three worlds. **First** the patina world of art,
literature and poetry, work, life, culture exists in itself for itself and
which we think can change, but which is without meaning and a
deception of various causes. It is all agency and no principal. The
first is absolutely assured the only reality. These people will swear
to you that the news is accurate, that all stars are stars. These are
the true believers in the JFK lone gunman, Sirhan Sirhan in front
of RFK not a bullet from behind, MLK lone gun, Twin Towers
terrorism, Sandy Hook elementary. Any question of this to first
levelers will produce paroxysms of hate as they try to choke the
life out of you. There is no discussion between the first and second
layers.

The First doesn't like to hear its stars are devils, but in the **Second**
deep under reality manipulated by the elite councils where wars are
decided ahead, and the winner pays the debts of the loser and
Stalin is an English agent, which goes on and on from the polio
cancer vaccine, Antarctica/Atlantis, moon landings, politicat
assassinations, underground cities, submarine bases under Kansas,

Blue Beam epigenetics, crisis actors, Bohemian groves, aluminum clouds: angelic princes that fell, metallic aerosolized fiberglass slices of microscopic cross section particles in clouds to fill lungs of nano tubules immersed in molten aluminum, all and more sponsored by the Prince Regnant Servitors, is most exposed by Levinas who says that all of our lives are organized around the hidden referent, not of the Shoah (Holocaust), but the Shoah to come of war. not a tumor in our memories, but a war now breaking our ribs for which we have no word. You can't read Levinas long without seeing that Difficult Freedom, Difficile Liberte, Totality and Infinity, Otherwise Than Being are dizzying reflections of height, or depth of the presentiment and memory of horror, w/o taking the holocaust of the past as a limited edition of the future. With the Nazi charges of subhuman ape and carrier of germs amplified to the useless eaters that British royalty thinks of the commoners of the world, the no time of Levinas past that he lives the rest of his life in a vigil of, endures his life "when one has that tumor in the memory...and death will no doubt cancel the unjustified privilege of having survived six million deaths. " That is the present of this past and a down payment in reverse, the past for the tumor of the future that nothing can cover over, even if we stand away from it in the present with out still everyday occupations, almost as if neither the past and its vertigo and the future that grips at our edge were never there, when both are the same. Past and future inhabit a non time, immemorial past and future, which have no memory and no prediction, but have in common a search for a language dedicated to the memory of those who died, or will, but without naming it as such, so that it is no theme for the news or discussion of any kind. Leave the present nameless, for if it fails to name itself. Why should we help it? It is too eager to name. We deny it space and we deny it time. It is

Destruktion that makes every mountain and hill of morals made low, a perfect recasting of the human without empathy, palaces, flags, magistrates tempests raging in shipwrecks so the murderer can see its sanction of the world with a clear conscience, but the providence and benevolence of the Father and the sacrifice of the Son to redeem all of us, wraps completely around this and opposes the underground. Herein we have all Value in itself because of His creation in us!

How much more delicious this is can bring in Che, who also had his hair lifted after a fashion, as it has been said in *A History of Che Guevara's Hair*, where "two women who lifted up in a basket," from *Zechariah* 5.9 where *two women* flying toward us, "gliding on the wind had wings like a stork, and they *picked up* the *basket* and flew into the sky" with Che Guevara's hair. This might as well describe the state of Scalia's body. The DNA of Che's hair taken from the mausoleum in Santa Clara, Cuba compared with his DNA "body" had more evidence than Scalia's DNA, when his body was first reported to have been cremated in El Paso, then that report was canceled and replaced with reports of a viewing by his family in his home state. It's a good thing this is invisible.